MW00329699

Mist at the Beach House

A Beach House Mystery, Volume 1

Victoria LK Williams

Published by Sun, Sand & Stories Publishing, 2020.

Mist at the Beach House

A Beach House Mystery-1

By

Victoria LK Williams

Copyright 2020

MIST AT THE BEACH HOUSE

First edition. March 31, 2020.

Copyright © 2020 Victoria LK Williams.

ISBN: 978-1393527022

Written by Victoria LK Williams.

To my hubby, who lets me dream

A BEACH HOUSE MYSTERY - 1

MIST
AT THE BEACH HOUSE

Victoria LK Williams

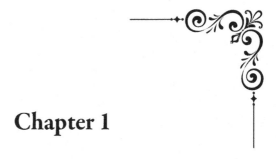

Chapter 1

M organ Seaver looked around her, taking in the sights, and felt a great weight lifted from her shoulders. A weight she wasn't aware she carried. The sound of children's laughter faded into the distance as she became focused on the island in front of her. Morgan always experienced a longing to be by the sea. But right now, her longing was for the island. And she didn't know why. She felt called in many ways that had nothing to do with the letter she had gotten from her aunt, beseeching her to come and help her with her library full of ancient books in need of desperate repair.

Morgan thought back to the letter and how it had arrived at the most appropriate time. She was in between jobs and getting restless, as she often did. Since she graduated from high school, Morgan had wandered the Atlantic Coast, looking for something, but not knowing what she was looking for. Her skill and talent at restoring old books had earned her a reputation, making the most exclusive libraries and private collectors call for her services. But when the letter from her aunt came, Morgan knew she needed to help. It was more than the family thing; it was a calling she'd been waiting for and hadn't known.

"Excuse me," called out a childish voice, and Morgan looked up quickly to see a beach ball heading her way. Quickly ducking out of the ball's path, she laughed with the child and picked up the ball, tossing it back to him.

"Thank you, Miss." The child started to run away but then seemed to remember his manners and turned back to call out to Morgan. She waved her hand in acknowledgment.

The interaction with the child brought her focus back to the here and now, and she looked around the beach area and noticed many children around the same age as the young boy with the beach ball happily playing. Mothers were grouped together, watching their children, and picnics were laid out on the crystal white sands of the beach. It was one of those beautiful days in late April when it wasn't too hot in the Florida sun. The winter crowd had thinned out as well, with most of the tourists starting to make their way back home to the northern states where the temperatures were finally beginning to climb. This time of year seemed to be a signal for the residents of the small coastal communities along the Florida peninsula that now was their time to take over the beaches.

The ringing of a small bell caught Morgan's attention, and she looked over towards the main road, noticing several bicyclists. A wide range of bikes made up the group of bikers, and she smiled at the tandem bike with two older people riding together. Her aunt's letter had warned her that biking, walking, and golf carts were the most common forms of transportation on the island. This suited Morgan just fine. She was anxious to get her car parked permanently and get to work.

"Standing here admiring the view won't get me there any faster." She laughed to herself. With one final look at the water, Morgan shrugged her shoulders and turned to walk back to the parking area where she had left her car.

Once in the car, she took a quick swig of cold water and then pulled out her aunt's notes to follow the directions that would lead her to the family home she would now call hers. Morgan didn't really need the instructions; the way home seemed instinctive. She could visualize the house that had been in the family for generations, and she remembered

4

her time as a child playing in the same sands as the children she'd just left. Her memories were clear, mixed with pictures in her mind of her mother and her aunt spending time with her along the beach.

Quickly glancing at the directions, she put the paper back down next to her and started towards the island. It was a one-way road over the island, and she waited patiently for a car coming across the bridge before she could take her turn to enter Pearl Island. Her car passed over the water as she made her way onto the island, and she experienced a profound sense of homecoming.

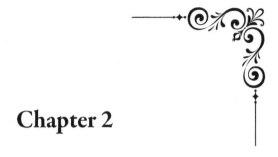

Chapter 2

With the memories guiding her, it didn't take long before her aunt's historic beach house could be seen in the distance. The house was three stories, and in all truth was the focal point of the island. It could be seen from almost any position on the island as if it was standing tall and strong guarding against something.

Morgan's feeling of homecoming intensified as she got closer to the house. When she reached the driveway, she stopped. Rather than pulling up towards the house, she got out of the car and just stood looking at the beautiful home. She knew the house had been in the family for close to a century, but it didn't show the ravages of time or weather. Her Aunt Meredith kept the house in beautiful repair, and her gardens, which surrounded the home, were a horticultural delight. Tropical blooms could be seen from the roadway, and foliage of assorted greens and textures filled the planting beds. There were no structured hedges around this house, everything had a natural flow to it, as if one with nature.

Morgan's eyes followed the path of a seagull soaring above the waves to perch itself on the balcony of the third floor of the house before her. The corners of Morgan's smile tugged into a smile as memories of playing in that third floor came flooding back. It had always been her favorite part of the house, and her Aunt Meredith had let her have free reign to play where she wanted whenever she visited.

"Well, you've arrived," Morgan told herself. "Standing here staring isn't going to get you settled. Let's get a move on, girl."

Getting back into the car, Morgan pulled up to the front walkway of the house. Reaching across the front seat, she grabbed her backpack and laptop, planning to come back out for her suitcases later. Right now, she wanted to get inside and find her aunt.

"Hello?"

Morgan slowly opened the front door, not concerned that it was unlocked as her aunt had reminded her the doors were never locked. Silence greeted her, and she was puzzled; her aunt had promised to be here when she arrived. Making her way into the hallway, Morgan set her bags down next to the stairway as the old grandfather clock chimed the arrival of the half-hour. Surprised, she glanced at her watch and saw that it was indeed half-past two. Morgan had made good time on her drive to the southern part of the state.

She moved as if guided by an old memory and made her way down the hallway to the kitchen. The smell of fresh-baked cookies greeted her, and there was a huge bouquet of wildflowers sitting in an old mason jar in the middle of the table. But there was no Aunt Meredith.

Walking over to the large French doors that opened up onto a path leading to the beach, Morgan's searched the horizon.

"There you are. I should have known you'd be along the shore," she mumbled to herself as she saw the silhouette of a woman walking close to the waves breaking on the shore.

Grinning to herself with excitement, Morgan opened the door and headed down the path to meet her aunt and reconnect after years of being apart.

"OH, MY GOODNESS, JUST look at you. You look just like a Seaver!"

Meredith Seaver had turned and watched her niece walk towards her across the sea dunes. Her voice called out to Morgan before she even reached her aunt's side, the pride evident in her tone.

MIST AT THE BEACH HOUSE

Morgan laughed outright at her aunt's words and, without thinking, raised her hand to push her jet-black hair out of her face, her jet-black hair with a streak of deep blue that she had put in on a lark, just to be different. She could put money on it that none of her relatives past or present had ever had hair like this.

"Really? Even with this?" she asked her aunt with a laugh.

"Yes, even with that brilliant blue streak. But you know each of us Seavers have had something unique about us that makes us stand out from the rest of the crowd."

"Even my mother? I rather doubt that, Aunt Meredith." Morgan shook her head in disbelief to her aunt's words. Then her disbelief turned to shock when her aunt answered her.

"Yes, even your mother. Did you know she had a birthmark? It's in the shape of a seashell right underneath her hairline on the back of her neck."

Morgan looked at her aunt with interest; she'd never known about the birthmark, and somehow it made her mother seem just a little less perfect. Then she shrugged her shoulders.

"Well, not to worry. This blue paint will fade shortly and I'll go back to being boring old me," she informed Meredith.

But her aunt just smiled at her, not saying a word as if she knew some secret.

Morgan made a move forward, ready to give her aunt a warm hug. But before she could take a step, her aunt turned away as if she hadn't seen the movement and swept her arms out towards the sea.

"It's time you came back to the island, Morgan. The sea knows you're here, and things are now in motion."

"I'm sorry, I don't know what you mean by that."

"You will. Things have already been set in motion. But for now, why don't you go back to the house and make yourself at home?"

"Aren't you coming?"

"Not right this moment. There are a few things I need to do. Go on and explore the house, pick out which room you want. There's snacks in the fridge, and if you feel up to it, the library is there for you to look over."

Morgan gave her aunt a funny look, surprised that Meredith wouldn't come up to the house with her. But her aunt simply blew her a kiss and turned and walked towards an outcropping of rocks. Morgan remembered from her youth these were an excellent place for hide-and-seek.

"Okay, Aunt Meredith, I'll talk to you when you get back to the house. And thank you for welcoming me home," Morgan called out to the woman as she walked away.

Meredith raised her hand, acknowledging the words, but she didn't turn around. Morgan watched the woman walk away until she went around the rocks and was lost from sight. Then with a shrug, she turned and made her way back towards the house, eager for the snack, and even more eager to reacquaint herself with her childhood home and to explore the vast library.

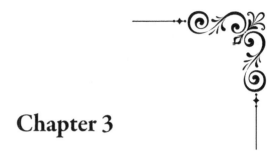

Chapter 3

E ven though Morgan was eager to explore the house and settle herself into the library, she got the mundane things completed first. Grabbing a cookie off the plate on the kitchen counter as she walked through, Morgan made her way to the front door. Picking up her backpack and bag, she headed up the stairs. She skipped the second floor and went straight to the third floor, where she found the room that she had claimed in her youth.

The room had always felt magical to her, like she was a princess stuck away from reality, waiting for Prince Charming to come and rescue her. But life quickly taught Morgan that there was no Prince Charming and that she had to rescue herself. It felt good to walk through the threshold of the room that held so many sweet memories from her childhood. She looked around the room and saw fresh flowers on the dresser and smiled to herself. It seemed Aunt Meredith had remembered this was her favorite room as well, and prepared it for her, even though she told her she would have her pick of the rooms.

Tossing her backpack on the bed, Morgan walked over to the window and looked out across the sand dunes and watched the waves come onto the shore. It was mesmerizing, but she quickly pulled herself away from that view and walked over to a door she remembered from her youth. Throwing the door open, she walked out onto the widow's walk that many of the old houses had on the island. This walkway went across the roofline. Decades ago, brides waiting for their sailors to come home would go to the widow's walk and look out over the ocean waiting for the ships to come in, bringing home their true loves. "Well, hello there. Are you the same bird I saw earlier?" Morgan spoke to a fat seagull that sat on the railing and then laughed at herself, knowing the seagull would not answer.

Deciding now would be the perfect time to get the rest of her bags in from the car while she still had the energy, and before she got involved in any of the library books, Morgan raced down the stairs and out to her car. It only took two trips to empty the car, and most of what she brought in went to her room. There was one large bag that she left at the base of the stairs. She would need to talk to her aunt before she decided where to place the tools of her trade. Her pressing box was still in the car, its heavy frame a little too bulky to bring in and take up room in the hallway. She could wait on that.

Looking around the first floor, she realized Meredith had not returned yet. When her stomach rumbled in protest of lack of food, she took her aunt up on her offer of a sandwich and made her way back to the kitchen. Grabbing a cold bottle of water from the fridge, she picked up the plate with her lunch and made her way to the porch. The porch was a wraparound and would connect to the front of the house. Meredith had old wicker rocking chairs scattered around the porch along with a comfortable table, chairs and lounges. She'd arranged the furniture so you could look out to the ocean no matter where you sat. From here, you could watch the approach of visitors coming to call. No matter where you looked, it felt comfortable and welcoming. Morgan gave a sigh of contentment as she settled into one of the large chairs, curling her feet underneath her and biting into her sandwich. Finishing her quick meal, Morgan knew it would be easier to just settle in deeper to the chair and take a quick nap, but she resisted the temptation and made her way back into the house.

When she entered the library, it caught her breath. It was much more than she remembered. Morgan walked around the room, running her fingers reverently along the spines of the books on the shelves, and inhaling the mustiness of the old pages and their stories deeply. There was a massive desk in the center of the room, and Meredith had placed comfortable chairs in convenient corners with reading lamps positioned to give a reader perfect lighting.

"Now, this is my idea of heaven." Morgan couldn't wipe the grin off her face as she studied the books.

She quickly realized there was no rhyme or reason to their placement. They placed modern paperbacks in amongst books that looked to be easily 50 to 75 years old. Fiction and nonfiction were mixed together, and when she looked a little deeper, she even found personal photo albums squeezed in amongst the published books.

"Oh, Aunt Meredith, it looks like I have my work cut out for me here."

Even though her common sense told her she should categorize the books, she couldn't help but feel that the library was perfect the way it was. After all, it was a family library, not a public library, and she was sure if she followed the shelves of books, she would see history in front of her. She knew from experience that people bought books at different stages of their lives. The books within easy reach were probably the most recently purchased, and she knew the stack that stood on the desk were current publications.

She smiled as she looked at the spines, reading an assortment of genres ranging from western to romance. There was a smattering of science fiction, but predominately they were mysteries. There were also numerous books that she didn't recognize. They didn't appear to be published books, and when she pulled one of them off the shelf, she found they were personal journals.

"Now this is a find." Morgan hugged the book to her chest, realizing the journals were probably records from, and about, her family. Not wanting to overstep herself, she put the book back on the shelf, deciding she would wait for her aunt to give her direction on what books needed attention. From the looks of things, there were a lot of books that needed to have work done to them. Spines were broken, jackets dusty and faded, and some covers looked like they were ready to fall off. Yes, there was plenty of work here to keep Morgan busy for years.

Walking over to a pile of books on one small end table, she picked up one sitting on top. It was a book she'd wanted to read for a long time, and without even thinking, she walked over to a comfortable chair in a corner with a window next to it where she could look out over the ocean. Opening the cover of the book, she was quickly lost in the story.

REACHING OVER HER HEAD, Morgan turned on the reading light next to her. Her movement brought her out of the book, and she looked around her, surprised at how dark the room had gotten. She'd been lost in the story for well over two hours, and with a jolt, she realized she hadn't seen or heard her aunt return. Maybe she had and decided to give Morgan the chance to relax. But either way, Morgan put the book down and went in search of her aunt. She wanted to catch up with her and thank her once again for welcoming her back home.

"Aunt Meredith?" Morgan stood in the grand hallway calling out to her aunt, but there was no response. She searched the entire house, but Meredith was nowhere to be found. There was no evidence that she'd ever returned from the beach. Dusk was about to settle, and Morgan was growing concerned. Yes, her aunt knew her way around the island and was probably perfectly fine, but it seemed odd that she hadn't come back when she said she would, knowing that Morgan had just arrived.

Morgan hated to be indecisive, but she also hated waiting around. Grabbing her cell phone, she went to search for her aunt. Her aunt would probably scoff at her worries, but Morgan couldn't shake the feeling of unease that was overtaking her. Using the same door she had earlier, Morgan walked from the kitchen down over the sea dunes to the beach. The waves were calm, and there was just the slightest of breezes. She headed toward the rock outcropping where she'd last seen her aunt. As she got closer to the rocks, a mist began to develop, giving the beach an eerie feeling. She looked around her, realizing the mist was where she was standing and had not spread across the dunes. Hoping to find her aunt before the mist became a real fog, Morgan picked up her pace and quickly reached the rocks.

When she rounded the rocks, she was shocked to find a grouping of people standing clustered over something lying on the sand. The mist cleared just long enough for her to recognize that two of the people were police officers, and the third was a beautiful young woman about her own age. The woman turned and saw Morgan.

"She's the one that did it. I saw her!" The woman lifted her arm and pointed in Morgan's direction, and the others took a step away from each other, staring at Morgan.

Their movements allowed Morgan to see what they had been staring at, and she gasped. The mist moved but not before Morgan saw the body of Meredith lying prone at their feet.

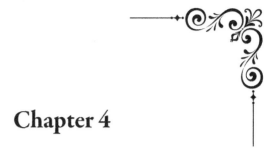

Chapter 4

M organ was torn. Her immediate reaction was to rush forward, but there was something in their stance that also made her want to turn and run back to the safety of her aunt's house. There was something about the way they were staring at her that made Morgan want to seek shelter and safety.

Her first instinct won out, and she stepped forward, not wanting to believe it was her Aunt Meredith on the ground. The others watched her walk towards them but stopped her before she got too close.

"I'm positive I saw her with Meredith; she is the one that killed her!" insisted the younger woman once again, pointing at Morgan.

The two officers look from the woman to Morgan, and the man took a step in Morgan's direction. As he did, he reached behind him and pulled out a pair of handcuffs, but his partner stopped him with a single word.

"Wait."

"Wait? Why would you wait? That's your killer—arrest her." The younger woman turned to the female cop, astonished they were not putting handcuffs on Morgan.

The other woman gave a shake of her head in caution.

"Let us do our job. We'll take statements from both of you. Right now, everybody needs to just calm down." The female officer put her hands up as if to stop the aggression of the other woman.

Morgan didn't know where to turn. Her eyes were drawn to the body before darting back and forth between the people in front of her.

Then the mist deepened as if to cover Meredith from Morgan's sight. The male officer gave a shudder of his shoulders as something cold draped across them. His partner stepped forward and put her hand on Morgan's arm, steering her away from the body.

"You're Meredith's niece, aren't you? It's Morgan, right?" she asked as she guided Morgan away.

Morgan looked at the officer and realized she was trying to take her mind off what was going on. By now, other police officers were arriving on the scene, the area was being roped off with evidence tape, and the gurney was being brought down the dunes, led by the coroner. Morgan felt tears develop. With head bowed, she stepped away from the scene in front of her, following the guidance of the officer.

"Yes, I'm Morgan Seaver. I don't understand this. I just talked to my aunt a couple of hours ago. She was supposed to come back up to the house, but time got away from me, and I didn't realize she hadn't come back. I was just coming down to look for her, and that's when I... I found you all."

The officer gave her a sharp look as if surprised by something Morgan had said. But she seemed to decide to not ask questions, at least not the questions obviously on her mind, and instead, she introduced herself to Morgan.

"It's okay, Morgan. We'll get this all sorted out. My name is Jenny White. I've known your aunt for years, and my partner is Stanley Newman. He's a relative newcomer to the island, but we won't hold that against him." Jenny was trying to put Morgan at ease, adding a bit of chitchat. By now, they had walked away from the other two, and Morgan turned to look over her shoulder to find the young woman her own age staring at her intently.

"And who's that? The one who is so positive I killed Meredith."

"Sirena Storm. She is relatively new to the island as well, but with strong family ties. Don't let her get to you. Once we take everybody's statements, we can figure out how your aunt died."

MIST AT THE BEACH HOUSE

The mist swirled around the two women, but Jenny ignored it. Morgan expected to feel the surrounding dampness, but it wasn't like any other mist she'd ever been in. It almost had a warm, comforting feeling to it, but it dissipated as Jenny and Morgan made their way back to the house.

"Stanley will be along in a moment. He'll take Sirena's statement first."

"She's not coming up to the house, is she?" Morgan asked sharply.

"No, there's no reason for her to. Besides, right now, she seems a little too aggressive towards you. I think she should keep her distance. Maybe once all this is sorted out, you too can start out again on the right foot, but for now, I think distance is a good thing to put between you."

They had reached the kitchen door, and with the familiarity of somebody who had been to Meredith's house many times, Jenny opened the door and guided Morgan into the kitchen. Not asking permission, she walked to the kitchen cupboards and pulled out two coffee mugs, keeping her back to Morgan as she got her own grief under control. Then Jenny walked over to the coffee maker, and flipped it on, like she knew it would be ready to brew. And she did; Jenny had spent many afternoons sitting in the kitchen with Meredith, catching up on the island gossip. And lately, all Meredith could talk about was the arrival of her niece. She had no fear or foreboding in her voice when she spoke about Morgan, and Jenny had a hard time believing her niece could show up at the island and immediately killed her aunt. It made no sense to the officer.

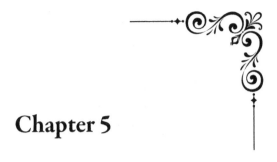

Chapter 5

Morgan wasn't even aware that she picked up the coffee cup and started to drink until the hot coffee scalded her lips. It seemed to be just what she needed to bring her out of her daze, and she looked across the table to see Jenny staring at her intently.

"Jenny, what's going on?"

"That's what we need to find out. Talk me through your day. What time did you get to the island, and what did you do when you got here?"

Morgan did as Jenny directed and quickly outlined what she had done all day. It didn't take long because she hadn't really done much. She had spent most of her time driving to get to the island. When she reached Pearl Island, she'd made a quick stop to fill up her gas tank, grab a drink, and then she had wandered down to the beach. After that, she waited her turn to cross over the one-lane bridge and then arrived at her aunt's house.

"And it was after 2 o'clock that you went down to the beach and talk to your aunt?"

"Yeah, I'm positive. I looked at the clock before I walked down to the shore. It surprised me no one was here because I knew she was expecting me. Then I remembered how much my aunt loved to walk the beach, so I figured that's where she went. And sure enough, that's where I found her."

"Positive about that time?"

Morgan looked at the officer sitting across from her, wondering why the time was so important, and she nodded her head in affirmation.

"Okay, that seems pretty matter-of-fact. Do you think there's anybody that could collaborate your story?"

"Well, yes, the cashier at the gas store. Wait a minute, I can do better than that. I have the receipt from the gas. I put it on my credit card. I bet that will say what time I purchased the gas."

"That's great, Morgan. If you'll hand it to me, I'll keep it for evidence."

"Evidence? Why do you need evidence against me?"

"Because Sirena was adamant that she saw you kill your aunt. We need that receipt to disprove her claim and clear your name."

Morgan understood Jenny's point and, reaching across the table, grabbed her purse that was sitting on the counter. Digging through her wallet, she pulled up the receipt and started to hand it to Jenny. She hesitated a moment and then grabbed her phone and took a quick picture of it. Then she looked at the officer apologetically.

"I'm sorry, it's not that I don't trust you. But I don't know you, and I just got to this island and found my aunt murdered and somebody trying to pin it on me. This is for my protection."

Jenny looked at Morgan with respect. Meredith had always told her that her niece was smart as a whip, street-savvy. Morgan had just proved her aunt's words to be true.

Before either woman could say another word, there was a knock on the door, and before they could answer, it was opened to reveal Jenny's partner, Stanley. Behind him was another man, one that Morgan vaguely recognized from her past. But it wasn't until he spoke that she remembered him.

"Morgan, I'm so sorry I wasn't there for Meredith. But I'm here now to help you in any way I can."

It was hard not to see the anguish in the older man's eyes. He was hard hit by Meredith's death, and Morgan remembered that he and her aunt had been close, rarely apart from each other. She had often seen him when she visited her aunt, and the woman had often talked about Dylan, both in her letters and when they spoke on the phone. Suddenly Morgan felt like she had a friend in her corner. Without waiting for Morgan to answer, Dylan pulled a chair up next to her and reached over to grab her hand and give it a reassuring squeeze. Then he looked over at Jenny and Stanley.

"What are you two doing about finding Meredith's murderer?"

Stanley popped his chest out as if insulted and pointed his finger at Morgan.

"Well, according to an eyewitness, this here is our murderer. She was seen at the crime."

"Umm, Stanley, I think we have a problem with our timeline. Did you speak to the coroner before you left?"

Jenny stood up and faced her partner, trying to get him to shut up before he said anything more to make himself look foolish.

"Yeah, I spoke to him briefly. Why?"

"Did he give you an approximate time of Meredith's death?"

Three sets of eyes turned to Stanley as they waited for his answer. Jenny had a good idea what he would say, but she needed him to say it out loud so the others could hear it.

"As near as he can figure it without examination, the coroner's placing the death sometime early this morning. Approximately 6 AM."

"That's what I thought too. Basing it just on the tides, there was no way Meredith's body had been there any earlier without being pulled out to sea, as close as it was to the shore. Besides that, Morgan has proof that she arrived on the island this afternoon, not this morning."

"Then who did Sirena see? She insists she saw someone bent over the body, and when Morgan Seaver showed up at the beach, she was quick to identify her. Sirena would have no reason to lie," Stanley countered.

While Stanley had been talking, Dylan had been getting paler and paler by the minute. Morgan looked at him, wondering what was going on, but he gave a slight shake of his head. It didn't take much for her to realize he didn't want to talk in front of the two police officers, and she wondered what was bothering him.

Morgan turned her attention back to the two officers who were quietly talking amongst themselves. Something clicked; the timeline made little sense. There was no way she could have spoken to her aunt if the coroner placed the time of her death early in the morning. He had to be wrong. She started opening her mouth to dispute the coroner, but once again, Dylan caught her attention and mouthed the word 'no.' Morgan raised her eyebrows at him, but self-preservation kicked in, and she kept her mouth closed. Jenny might be on her side, but she felt like Stanley was opposed to her being in the clear. He wanted to believe Sirena over the facts. And if she were to believe the facts as well, then when she had spoken to her aunt after her death. How was this even possible?

Chapter 6

It appeared Stanley needed to feel self-important. He made Morgan go through her entire timeline once again, even though Jenny had written everything down. The man could have easily looked at her notes to find his answers. It was clear he was trying to discover a way that Morgan had gotten to the island, killed Meredith, and then backtracked so Sirena saw her. He was about to go through the whole process again when Jenny stood up, shaking her head.

"Enough, Stanley. Morgan has gone through this more times than she needs to, and she's never varied from her account. There are other things that you and I need to do rather than sitting here, putting Morgan through this again. Let the poor girl come to grips with her aunt's death."

Stanley stuttered and stammered, offended that his partner had cut him off. But Jenny didn't budge, and she held the door open, motioning for Stanley to go. After he walked out the door, she turned back to Morgan and Dylan.

"I can't tell you two how sorry I am about Meredith's death. She was a good friend, to most of the people on this island and to me. We will deeply miss her. Dylan?"

"Yes?"

"Are you staying here with Morgan?"

Dylan glanced at Morgan before he answered, noting that the younger woman was looking dazed and exhausted.

"Yes, if Morgan doesn't mind, I'll stay here. There are things we need to talk about. Things Meredith would want her to know and do."

"Good. Morgan, I don't want you to feel afraid, but I also don't want you to be on your own, at least until you get a feel for the island and our citizens. Someone murdered your aunt, and without the guidance of somebody who knows who's who, you could step into danger."

Jenny looked back and forth between the two and came to a decision. "Dylan, you call me if anything, and I mean anything, seems out of the ordinary. Out of the ordinary for this island." Jenny didn't stay any longer, ignoring the confused look Morgan gave her. Dylan would be the one to answer her questions, and that's the way it should be. But right now, Jenny had to calm her partner down before he started more trouble than he knew he was getting into. And one of the first things she wanted to investigate was just who Sirena really was.

Silence filled the kitchen after the two police officers left. Both Morgan and Dylan seemed lost in their own thoughts. Thoughts about Meredith. It was Dylan who broke the silence first. Reaching across the table, he grabbed Morgan's hands and gave them a gentle squeeze.

"I failed your aunt. I'm so sorry, Morgan. I wasn't there when she needed me."

Morgan looked up from her coffee with surprise at his words, and she hastened to assure him she didn't hold him responsible for the actions of somebody else against her aunt.

"Oh, Dylan, there's no way you would have known somebody would kill Aunt Meredith. No more than I could. If I had known, I could've been here so much earlier, and maybe I could've prevented it. No, there are just some things in life that happen that you have no control over."

Dylan gave a slight nod of agreement and was silent for a few moments, as if carefully picking out his next words.

"Meredith was so looking forward to seeing you. There were so many things she wanted to tell you, things she wanted to show and teach you. I think she knew there was trouble brewing."

"What do you mean, trouble brewing? Wasn't this a random act of violence? How could she predict this?"

His statement surprised Morgan, but he didn't answer her right away. Morgan was getting an uneasy feeling when he finally broke the silence.

"Let me ask you a question. Have you noticed that your visits down here have been longer each time, and you've been more reluctant to leave?"

Morgan gave Dylan a curious look, wondering what he was getting at. Rather than answering, she just gave a shrug of her shoulders, and he continued.

"You know your aunt shares a lot with me, and I couldn't help but notice as you were taking on new jobs that you were slowly but surely working your way from the north to the south. And you always took jobs near the ocean."

"Have I? It wasn't intentional. It's just the way the jobs came—"

"But you turned away jobs for out west or in the middle of the country. Whether you realize it or not, you were following a family calling to come home."

Morgan shook her head, wondering if the shock of Meredith's death had affected Dylan more than he realized. This all sounded way too hokey for her, and she protested, but he continued not letting her get a word in edge-wise.

"Before you dismiss my observation, you need to see something." Getting to his feet, Dylan motioned for Morgan to follow him out of the kitchen. She pushed her chair back and indulged the older man, following him down the hallway that led to her aunt's study. Dylan walked in first, turned the overhead light on, and then pointed to the corkboard Meredith had set up behind her desk. It was a map of the

United States from Maine to Florida. Meredith had put push pins in the map all along the coastline, and when Morgan stepped forward, she saw they were places where she had worked over the last few years. She looked at Dylan and then back at the map, surprise registering on her face.

"I never realized it. But you're right; I have stayed close to the ocean."

"And each of your jobs has been getting shorter and shorter, as if you're being pulled down here. Didn't you feel that, Morgan? Didn't you feel the pull to come to the island?"

Morgan stepped away from the corkboard, not sure how she wanted to answer Dylan. To be honest, his intensity was making her nervous. Too much had happened today to deal with something else.

Dylan saw her reaction and hastened to reassure her he wasn't crazy.

"These were all things your aunt was going to tell you. Maybe I'm speaking out of turn, or maybe I'm saying things too soon, but we need to talk about what's going on. For now, let's just concentrate on getting you settled in. This is your home now, Morgan."

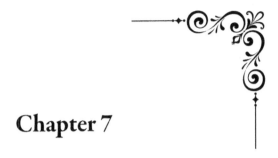

Chapter 7

Dylan's words hung in the air. Morgan had never called a place home before, but as soon as he said it, she knew it was true. The island was now her home, and whether her aunt intended to leave it to her or not, the Seaver house was now hers. She was the last Seaver alive. Her mother had died years before in a tragic accident not far off the coast from where the Seaver house stood, looking out over the ocean. Meredith had never told Morgan the full details of her mother's death, and she had never asked. As the knowledge of being the last of her family penetrated, Morgan knew she had responsibilities that needed to be taken care of, starting with her aunt. She looked at Dylan, and it was as if he could read her mind. He smiled sadly before he spoke.

"There's nothing that you need to worry about Morgan. Meredith made sure that all her final plans were made. She didn't want you to have to deal with anything. The only thing she really wanted was to make sure that you would feel at home here and stay. I'm going to leave now. But if you open the desk drawer, you'll find your aunt left you some letters in case of an emergency. I'll be back later. In the meantime, stick close to the house. There is a killer loose, and you may not know who friend or foe is."

Dylan gave her shoulders a squeeze in comfort and encouragement, then pointed at the desk with one hand and with the other got a key from his pocket. "This is my key. Your aunt has another copy on her key ring, but she insisted I have a copy too. You'll understand more when you read the letters, and I'm sure you'll have tons of questions for me.

I'll bring dinner when I return, and we can sit and talk. I'll answer as many of your questions as I can."

Without giving Morgan a chance to say anything, Dylan pressed the key into the palm of her hand and then left. Morgan wondered what she would find in the desk. Part of her was curious; the other part was anxious. Staring at the desk, she knew it contained some of her answers and probably more questions. She found she was eager to know, even postmortem, a little bit more about her aunt.

Shrugging her shoulders to fight her hesitation, Morgan walked around to sit in the grand chair behind the desk. The chair was perfect for a queen and was comfortable. The desk was hand-carved, beautifully ornate, and when she looked closely, she saw that the engravings were of mermaids and sea creatures, and she wondered who had done such beautiful work.

"Sitting here staring at the desk isn't going to find my answers. Use that key and unlock it, girl." Morgan scoffed at herself. This was a habit she often had, talking to herself. Maybe it was because, in her profession, she was alone most of the time, and she needed to hear the sound of her own voice.

Taking a deep breath, Morgan used the key and unlocked the drawer. Pulling it open, she saw inside three envelopes and two jewelry boxes. Two of the envelopes looked official in their legal size, sealed with an old-fashioned wax seal. But it was the third envelope that caught Morgan's attention. She recognized her Aunt Meredith's elegant handwriting, and she knew without even touching it that she would find it was a personal letter to her. Like a child wanting to save the best candy for last, she pushed the envelope to the side and reached for the jewelry boxes. She was curious because she couldn't remember seeing her aunt wear anything other than a ring, and the ring was vague in her memory; she just knew that her aunt always wore it. She flipped the lid of the larger flat box and gasped at the beauty lying in the black velvet insides of the box. She had never seen a more perfect set of pearls in her life, but they weren't the traditional white pearls. No, these were a mixture of colors: white, gray, black, pink, and every other color she'd ever seen in a pearl. The box held the highest quality of each of those colors, gathered and strung together to create this masterpiece. Reverently, she picked them up out of the box and held them against her throat. She instantly felt a sense of peace, and when she pulled the pearls away, her throat felt warm where they had laid. Looking at the box, she saw there was a matching bracelet. She placed the necklace back in the box and reached for the smaller ring size box.

Before Morgan could open the box, something caught her eye outside the window. It was a slight movement, and she turned to find herself staring into the beautiful brown eyes of a longhaired tabby kitten on the other side of the window. The animal had jumped up onto the windowsill and seemed to be watching Morgan's every movement.

"Funny, I don't remember Meredith having a cat. Poor thing's probably looking for some food."

Pushing the drawer closed, Meredith jumped to her feet, intent on finding the cat and making sure it had food and water. She'd always had a soft spot for cats, and she hoped this one was friendly, someone she could talk to in this big old house.

But by the time Morgan walked across her aunt's office to the French doors that led out to the patio, the cat had disappeared.

"Oh well, he'll come back if he's hungry," Morgan said to herself, but she couldn't help but feel disappointed.

As Morgan stood looking out into the courtyard, she swallowed and realized all the coffee she had drank had only made her thirstier, and the only cure for that was a cold drink of water. As she walked by the desk, she reached out and grabbed the envelope that had been written by her aunt. She could deal with the rest later, but somehow, she felt it was important she read this letter immediately. It was as if the letter beckoned her with its urgency, and Morgan hoped she would find answers she needed within her aunts words.

Chapter 8

Morgan made her way out the front door to sit on one of the rocking chairs on the wraparound porch. The overhang from the roof gave the porch plenty of shade, and the view of the ocean was enticing, but she had no interest in watching the sea at this moment. The letter was calling for her to open it. After taking a big swallow from her bottle of water, she set it down and picked up the envelope. As she felt the packet, she noticed there was a bulge within the papers, and she carefully opened the seal, not wanting to lose what was inside. She held her hand out and tipped the envelope so that the object would fall into her hand. She gasped at the beauty of the gem that sat gleaming back at her. She had never seen a more perfect pearl, nor one in this color; it was a beautiful hue of blue. Putting the papers down, she reached with her other hand and picked up the pearl, holding it up to the light to get a better look at it.

"Didn't even know a pearl would come in this color. It's beautiful." Then Morgan noticed that someone had drilled the pearl to go onto a necklace, and she felt sad for a second that they had marred the perfection. She carefully put the blue pearl in the envelope for safekeeping and then turned her attention to the papers sitting on her lap. Morgan recognized her aunt's penmanship. At the top of the page was the date and time, and she drew in a sharp breath. Meredith had written this to her just hours before her death.

'My sweet Morgan. I'm sorry that you must read this without me being around, but I know my time is up. There are so many things I want to tell you. But you should discover what is in store for you a little at a time. Otherwise, believe me, it will be overwhelming. You're not alone here on the island; you have friends here that will help guide your path. Listen to them, rely on them, but rely on your own intuition. I'm sending two special people to be with you. Don't be sad for me. I make this decision on my own; my actions are for the greater good. The good of our family and of protecting the island. All this, you will come to understand later."

Morgan shivered, and she looked around anxiously as if somebody was reading over her shoulder. But there was nobody around, and she dropped her eyes back down to the paper and continued reading.

"First is the pearl. Each member of the family is given a pearl by their predecessor. I have specifically chosen the blue one for you. The blue pearl stands for truth, intuition, trust, responsibility, tranquility, and courage. You will need these qualities in the times to come. There is a box of pearls in my desk underneath the velvet; you will find a chain. This is for your pearl. The chain may look delicate, but it is strong beyond measure, and it will keep your pearl safe. I have added my pearl to the necklace in the box, as each of our ancestors has added theirs. You'll know when the time is right to add yours. But that won't be for many, many years."

Morgan broke from her reading to gaze out at the sea. She was almost afraid to read the rest of the letter, but she must. She wanted to find anything she could that might help find her aunt's killer. Or tell her why Meredith had wanted Morgan to return to Pearl Island now, after so many years.

"In the other box, you will find a ring. I cannot tell you much about the ring; you need to discover its secrets for yourself. I will tell you this much: once you put the ring on, never take it off. You'll understand. There are so many other things that I need to tell you but there aren't enough lines on the page. Besides, you need to find out most of this on your own. I have left you all the resources you will ever need. You'll find most of them in the library. Your favorite place, if I remember correctly. I will always be with you, Morgan, in ways you will never know. But know this: both your mother and I loved you with all our hearts."

Morgan's eyes blurred with tears, and it surprised her when one of them dropped onto the paper, mixing with the ink. Morgan quickly used her shirttail and dabbed the water spot so it wouldn't ruin the paper. Then she promptly wiped the other tears on her face so they wouldn't drip on the paper and noticed the postscript added to the bottom of the page. Meredith had added it in haste without her usual perfect penmanship.

"Don't trust everybody who says they are your friend. There are a few who will be friends for life, but there will be those that will try to be friends only for their own gain. These people will be more dangerous than they appear. Take care, my sweet niece. Protect our island and have a great life."

Morgan's hands dropped to her lap, the paper still clutched in her fingers. It was clear her aunt was trying to warn her about something, but what? And why had she willingly walked into danger? It was clear she knew something would happen to her, so why didn't she ask for help? Morgan sat there staring out at the ocean, gently rocking in the rocking chair without even realizing she was making the movements. It was a faint meow that she heard coming from inside the house that drew her attention.

Wondering if it was the same cat she'd seen earlier, she got to her feet and walked back into the house, following the soft cries of the cat back to her aunt's office. But when she looked around the room, there was no cat. However, the desk drawer was partly open, and Morgan knew she had closed it tightly. Folding papers back into the envelope, she took out the pearl and walked over to the desk, eager to put it on its chain and then put it on. Once the pearl was around her neck, Morgan closed the box with the pearl necklace of many colors. She dropped her aunt's notes down on top of the other envelopes. Then she reached for the smaller box that contained the ring her aunt was so adamant she wear.

But when she opened the box, there was no ring inside. In haste, Morgan pulled the drawer out as far as it could go, searching for the ring, but it wasn't there. Then she remembered the drawer had been partly opened.

Had someone come into the house while she was sitting out front? Who had stolen her ring?

Chapter 9

Morgan frantically searched for the missing ring. She pulled out the other desk drawers looking in case it had fallen through the back half of the desk. She moved around the few knickknacks on the desktop, but to no avail. After crawling under the desk to see if it had fallen on the floor and coming up empty, Morgan searched in the most unlikely places she could think of. She looked under the leaves of the philodendron sitting by the desk, hoping maybe the ring had fallen off onto the top of the soil, but no luck. From there, she started searching the shelves, even the wastebasket, but the ring was nowhere to be found.

Exhausted, Morgan looked around the room wondering if maybe her aunt had just never put the ring inside the box, and instead, it was in a jewelry box somewhere else. She heard the meow of a cat and looked out into the courtyard just in time to see the tabby's tail swish around the corner. Morgan walked over to the door to call the cat to her. But when she opened the door and called, she heard no answering meow. Looking around the courtyard, it was clear to see that it was one of her aunt's favorite places. It was immaculate, with comfortable chairs in the shade and fragrant flowers in abundance. As her eyes traveled the garden, she noticed a bit of sand off to the side of the door. Stepping out onto the patio, she looked at the sand from a different direction and was astonished to find the sand had formed a footprint. Someone had been looking in the window and may have even come in through the door. Instead of being frightened, Morgan was furious. She had heard of people who came to homes and tried to steal things after somebody had died. It hadn't even been twenty-four hours and already, her aunt's privacy was being violated. Her temper rising, Morgan took a deep breath to calm herself.

"So that's the way it's going to be, huh? So much for a nice, safe little island. Well, they won't get in again; I will lock the doors from now on." Realizing she had spoken the angry words out loud, Morgan looked around as if expecting somebody to be there listening, but there was no one. Turning on her heel, she went back into the house, locking the door firmly behind her. She had searched every inch of the office, and there was no ring here. Her aunt's letterhead mentioned there were things in the library that she would need; that would have to be the next place she would search.

Morgan started out the door to head towards the library, but the phone rang before she had taken two steps. With a frustrated sigh, she turned back to the desk to answer the old-fashioned phone that sat there.

"Hi Morgan, it's Jenny. I just wanted to check and make sure you were okay. You've had quite a day." Morgan quickly thanked her and, still angry about the intrusion in her aunt's home, she told Jenny about the missing ring.

"Well, keep checking around the house. If you don't find it by tomorrow, we'll have to make a report out. Keep an eye out for anything else that might be disturbed. I realize you don't know if something is missing, but you might be able to tell if something has obviously been pushed out of place."

Morgan appreciated that Jenny didn't try to placate her and took her seriously. The officer was right; there was no way Morgan would know if something was missing unless it was apparent. But she intended to search anyway, and she promised to call the officer in the morning and let her know how she made out. Thanking Jenny for the call, Morgan hung up and started once again for the library.

But as she walked by the front door, she changed her mind. She had a desperate urge to walk along the dunes, taking the same steps her aunt had taken earlier. She didn't think about the possibility of the danger, only that she felt a call to the shore, a need to go out past the dunes.

Reaching up to touch the pearl hanging around her neck, she remembered her aunt's note and the traits of the Blue Pearl. Courage was one, and Morgan felt full of courage as she touched the pearl. Closing the door behind her, she used Dylan's key, locking it before heading down towards the dunes. Morgan walked without thought, soaking in the atmosphere. She felt at peace here, and she could remember her aunt saying it was the most wonderful spot on the earth. If it wasn't for her aunt's death, she would be inclined to agree with her.

As if her feet had a will of their own, Morgan made her way down towards the outcropping of rocks her aunt had disappeared behind. But she couldn't make herself walk any further than the rocks; she had no desire to see the spot where her aunt had laid. Instead, she climbed up on one of the lower rocks and sat, watching the waves crash against the shore. How long she sat there, she didn't know, but she noticed a mist beginning to develop. She watched it swirl around her, almost as if it was doing an ancient dance. She was so involved in watching her immediate area that she didn't realize the mist was getting thicker. Watching the movements of the mist, she swayed as if listening to music. It took a few moments, and then she realized she was listening to music, the distant sound of a haunting violin. Morgan quickly jumped off the rock, looking around her in surprise at how thick the mist had gotten. Suddenly she felt afraid as she realized the music was heading towards her.

"Trust him."

Morgan clearly heard the words, but she didn't know where they came from, and in a panic, she turned from the rock and hurried back towards the house. It should have been difficult going, but as she made her way, the mist seemed to clear enough to make a path for her to see. Climbing up over the dune to the stairs to the house, Morgan saw the mist was disappearing. Looking back behind her, she could see the form of somebody walking down the beach. They didn't seem to be coming towards her, but she still felt afraid and quickly unlocked the door, entering the house for its sanctuary.

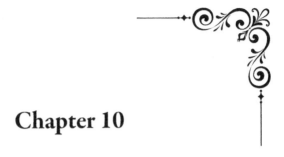

Chapter 10

M organ's hand automatically reached for the doorknob. But as she started to lock the door, she chastised herself.

"I don't know why you're so nervy. The poor guy was probably just walking along the beach practicing his music."

Laughing at herself, Morgan stepped away from the door. But at the last second, she turned back and locked it, remembering that somebody had made their way into Meredith's office.

Still feeling tensed and a little unnerved, Morgan made her way to the stairs and without thinking, up to the widow's walk. Opening the door, she stepped out, the breeze billowing her hair as the smells of salt and sea engulfed her. She looked out over the ocean and felt her nerves settle. The sea had always had that effect on her. Glancing down at the shore, she watched as the mist disappeared, thinking how odd it was that it showed up and disappeared randomly.

Meredith had placed a glider up against the wall of the house, providing shade and protection from the winds. Morgan sat in the overstuffed cushions to relax. She remembered sitting with her aunt as a child while they read one of the many books in the library. Her eyes blurred at the memory, and she could picture the book and how much her aunt had treasured it.

Brushing away an unshed tear, Morgan stared out past the railing, taking in the sight of the boat lights coming and going from the harbor as the sky dimmed with the approach of dusk. She saw the ferryboat on its last daily run coming in from the opposite end of the island.

"I can see most of the island from here. No wonder Aunt Meredith loved this spot so much. That can't be the same ferry from when I was a kid—it was old then." Talking out loud to herself, Morgan nestled deeper into the cushions, letting memories from her youth surface. She knew the ferryboat was the primary access to the commercial end of the island, and that it arrived at the island pier every four hours, weather permitting, during daylight. It could accommodate five cars at a time, which for the population of the island was perfect. Most tourists that visited the island came from the beachside, the same way Morgan had entered the island earlier.

A faint smile hovered over her lips as she remembered her childhood excursions with her aunt, taking the ferry the short distance from the island to the mainland for an afternoon of shopping or to catch the latest Disney movie in the theaters.

Morgan lost track of time, and it wasn't until she heard a faint sound coming from downstairs that she realized how late it was. Opening the door, she walked back into her room and could clearly hear the doorbell this time. There was something haunting about the six notes the doorbell played. Morgan knew she'd heard the tune before, but she couldn't figure out where; it was somewhere in the back of her mind, and it would come to her when she needed it. She thought it quaint that her aunt had picked a musical doorbell rather than the old-fashioned ding-dong doorbell.

Hurrying down the stairs, she rushed to the front door and opened it to find Dylan standing there. Behind him was a young man around her own age. His curly brown hair was windblown, and he had a warm smile on his face. Dylan held up packages of food for her to see and then nodded over his shoulder to the young man.

"I hope you don't mind; my nephew was with me, and I thought I'd bring him along. He was a great friend of your aunt's. Morgan, this is Gabriel."

Morgan smiled hesitantly but then held out her hand. After all, if he was a friend of her aunt's, then surely, he would be welcomed in the house. Gabriel shuffled his hands, and it took a moment for Morgan to realize what he held. As he held his hand out to shake hers, she stared at the violin gripped in his other hand.

"Was it you I heard earlier?" she asked him.

"Yes, and I'm sorry if I startled you. You ran off so quickly, I didn't have a chance to introduce myself. But I knew Dylan was coming back here for dinner, so I asked if I could join him. I can't tell you how sorry I am about Meredith."

Gabriel's tone was soft, and she could hear the sorrow in it. Yes, she was right; he had known and loved her aunt just as she and Dylan did.

"Of course, you're both welcome. Come on in. Dylan, that smells heavenly. I don't know what's in that bag, but I sure am anxious to get to it."

Stepping aside, Morgan waved her hand to welcome her guests into the house. With years of experience of having taken the same path, Dylan led the group towards the kitchen. Then he pulled the food out of the bags, the smell of Italian spices tickling her nose from the local pizza shop, while Gabriel walked to the cupboard and found some plates and glasses. A few minutes later, the three of them were sitting at the kitchen table, sharing a meal of fried chicken and mashed potatoes, and pie that Morgan was sure had been freshly baked, while they shared memories of Meredith.

They lost track of time as they talked and reminisced, Dylan filling Morgan in on some of the things her aunt had been doing recently. Most of it Meredith had told Morgan in her letters, but it was nice to hear from the friends who had shared the most time with her. He made Morgan feel just a tiny bit closer to her aunt.

When there came the inevitable gap in conversation that always happens, Gabriel brought up the subject of Sirena and her accusations against Morgan.

"You'll find out sooner or later, but there is a rift between the Seavers and a few other families on the island. It's not really a feud, just an uneasiness between the families that goes back for generations. Sometimes it flares up, and other times it just lays dormant. I have a feeling it's flaring up again; you and Sirena are the catalyst."

Morgan looked at Dylan, and he nodded his head in agreement. She had no idea what Gabriel meant, but she had felt the animosity from Sirena and knew it was more than just an accusation. It was deep-seated, something that couldn't be explained. Something that made her fearful.

"You can't possibly mean an old-fashioned feud like the Hatfields and McCoys?" Morgan tried to laugh at Gabriel's words, but it fell flat.

"No, it's darker than that," Dylan said. "You'll find out about everything as time goes on. But you're going to have to find out a lot of this on your own. Gabriel and I will be here to help you; we'll have your back."

Morgan shuddered at his words. Whether he meant to scare her or not, he had. Suddenly she had an urge to get away from the house and away from everyone.

Gabriel seemed to read her mind, and he pushed back his chair, holding his hand out to her. "Why don't we go for a walk? Have you seen anything other than the shore since your arrival?"

Morgan shook her head in answer to his question, and she got to her feet, ready to take him up on his offer.

"Do you want to come with us?" She looked at Dylan, who shook his head.

"No, the two of you go on ahead, I'll just clean up here and make a pot of coffee for when you get back. Gabriel, why don't you show Morgan the gardens? It will be a nice change for her."

Gabriel nodded in agreement and walked to the kitchen door, waiting for Morgan to join him.

Chapter 11

M organ followed Gabriel's lead when they left the house and followed the courtyard path in the opposite direction of the beach. It surprised her when he stopped at the small gate off the pathway.

"This is new since the last time I was here."

"Your aunt added it about a year ago. It leads to the community gardens. But you'll see in a minute that the private area your aunt owns has something more than just the gardens in mind. I won't say anything more. I want you to be surprised."

Morgan's surprise grew as she watched him enter a code to the lockbox on the gate.

"Now that is surprising. My aunt has never been security conscious."

"She put this in more for keeping people from coming off the pathway into her courtyard. It wasn't for security but more because she just wanted her privacy."

Holding the gate open, Gabriel motion for Morgan to go on ahead of him.

It only took a couple of steps to get into the thick of the garden. The dense canopy overhead dropped the temperature two degrees, making it a welcome relief from the setting sun. Orchids hung from the trees, and there was a sweet scent of something Morgan could not identify. The birds in the trees chattered to each other, and a small rabbit jumped in front of her. As the rabbit looked up at her, Morgan had an uneasy feeling that the rabbit would start saying, "I'm late, I'm late, I'm late! I'm late, I'm late. For a very important date. No time to say hello. Goodbye. I'm late, I'm late, I'm late," like the White Rabbit from *Alice In Wonderland*. But he just kept going across the pathway and disappeared into the brush. She smiled at her foolishness.

But then a strange cry echoed throughout the garden, making Morgan jump. She looked at Gabriel, but he said nothing, just motioned for her to continue. The path wandered through the garden. As it came around one curve, it opened, and Morgan stopped in her tracks, her mouth hanging open, looking at the sight before her.

"Oh my gosh, peacocks! There must be half a dozen of them here."

She stood watching the movements of the large birds and didn't see the smile Gabriel sent in her direction. The birds didn't seem to be afraid of the two intruders into the garden, and one magnificent male opened his tail feathers as if welcoming them to their domain. Morgan turned around to Gabriel, looking for an explanation.

"The peacocks started as a pair that your aunt adopted from an old friend. That was part of the reason she created this section of the garden. If we keep going forward, there's another gate that will prevent people from coming in and disturbing the peacocks. Of course, the birds come and go where they want, and it's not at all unusual for them to be in the public area as well. We have peacock-crossing signs on the roadway for the tourists to beware of. They're harmless; they've attacked nobody, and Meredith has always made sure that the birds had everything they needed."

Morgan burst out laughing. "Most people have pet parakeets but not my aunt. Everything is bigger, better, and more exotic with her."

Gabriel joined in her laughter, happy to see her forgetting her troubles for a moment.

"Once we get to the second gate, we will be in the public gardens. The garden club is responsible for the maintenance of the gardens in this area. It started out as a small project and has grown into something

46

wonderful for the island. It's a nice break from the beach once in a while."

Gabriel stepped forward to lead the way through the second gate. Morgan looked around before she followed him, noticing a few benches scattered in the area. She had a feeling her aunt had spent time here, and she looked forward to being able to do the same herself.

"Morgan?"

Morgan looked up and realized Gabriel was at the gate waiting for her. With one last look around, Morgan picked up her pace to meet him at the entrance. Once they were through the second gate, several pathways worked their way into the public gardens from different angles. She looked at Gabriel, wondering which one to take, and he just shrugged his shoulders.

"Take your pick. All the paths lead to the center of the garden. A large fountain and benches are there to sit and relax. The fountain has a little wading pool which the kids enjoy."

Morgan picked the pathway to the right, and together they started meandering through the beautiful plantings the garden club had created. As she walked, Morgan noticed it was very organized but still appeared to be a natural setting. They came around one corner, and the smell of herbs overwhelmed her senses. Gabriel explained that this was a community garden, and the herbs were for anybody to take a snipping of.

Their time in the garden was a quiet reprieve. They didn't run across anybody else; most people were probably home enjoying their dinners.

It was getting darker, and Gabriel suggested they head back. They'd only gone a short distance when they heard footsteps walking in their direction. Morgan instinctively slowed her pace and was glad she did when the burly figure came around the corner at a fast pace. It was Officer Stanley Newman, and a few steps behind him was his partner, Jenny Colbright.

It was Jenny who spoke first, reassuring them that everything was okay.

"We do a lot of foot patrol around here, and the garden is one of our main areas," she explained. "We've had no problems, but you never know when a couple of teenagers will want to use it as a make-out spot, or a tourist from the mainland decides it's a good spot to drink."

Morgan murmured in agreement and made to sidestep the other officer, but he wouldn't move. Instead, he put his hands on his hips and glared at her.

"Don't get too comfortable around here. I got my eye on you, and I'm gonna prove you killed your aunt."

Morgan took a step back, bumping into Gabriel, who put a steady hand on her arm. She took comfort from his touch and took a deep breath.

"You try, Officer Newman. But you're wasting your time. I did not kill my aunt. And anyone who says I did is mistaken."

Jenny quickly stepped in between the two of them to break the tension. Giving her partner a slight push toward another path, he had no choice but to move forward or continue the altercation. Even he knew he had no reason to stay, and Stanley glared at Morgan as he left.

"I don't know why he's so convinced you killed Meredith when all the evidence points otherwise. Just stay out of his way until he gets over this. That's the best advice I can give you. Morgan, I'm sure you're feeling overwhelmed, but I hope you feel the island can be your home when this is all cleared up."

Not waiting to hear if Morgan would answer her, Jenny followed her partner to make sure he didn't turn back. As they left, Morgan felt her hands tremble, surprised how much the man's accusations bothered her.

"Come on, let's head back to the house. Uncle Dylan will have that coffee ready by now."

MIST AT THE BEACH HOUSE

Gabriel's soft voice broke the silence, and with a nod of agreement, Morgan took the path towards the Seaver beach house.

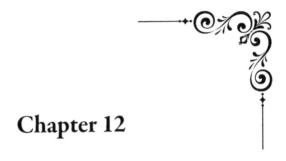

Chapter 12

The three of them finished the pot of coffee and a tray of cookies Dylan had found in the cupboard. They shared tears and laughter as they reminisced about their times with Meredith. But finally, the inevitable happened, and it was time for the two men to leave and for Morgan to face her first night in the Seaver house.

She closed and locked the door behind the men as they left, assuring them she was comfortable in the house by herself. She leaned against the door after they had left and was surprised to find she was comfortable in the house. She had no fears of being alone in her family home. There were too many good memories that she wanted to spend time with. And one of the first memories she would enjoy was the library.

With hurried steps, like a child rushing to open a gift, Morgan made her way to the library. This had always been her favorite spot, other than the widow's walk. Morgan was sure this was where her love for books started, here in Aunt Meredith's library. Her aunt had taught her to respect books, and to always be careful of their spines, not to dog-ear the pages, and to keep the shelves well dusted. That had been her childhood task, to dust the bookshelves, and as she grew older, Meredith had allowed her to climb ladders to reach the top shelves.

She marveled at the rows of old books lining the shelves. As a child, Morgan considered it a treat to be allowed to explore the books. Often, she didn't understand what was written, but there were beautiful pictures within the old pages. It was during one of her many visits that

Morgan decided the occupation of preserving books was her calling. She taught herself how to repair books, and then when it was time for college, she picked a school to learn the fine art of book repair. From there, she'd been able to create a business; she categorized private libraries, called into authenticity first editions, and repaired old books often neglected and unwanted within private collections. Her work had taken her to some of the most illustrious homes along the Eastern seaboard. She even worked for some more specialized private libraries and had built up a good reputation. A reputation that made her sought after by not only private collectors but by auction houses, as well.

Morgan looked through the shelves. There was one book she was searching for, an old favorite from when she was a child. It was a children's book with no particular meaning, except it was one her mother had written and illustrated. It was one of the few memories Morgan had of her mother.

"There you are."

Morgan felt a sense of relief as she reached out and grabbed the book off the shelf. Now she really felt like she'd come home. She knew there were journals, some decades old, filled with the recordings of events about the island and her family, and she had every intention of looking through them. But for now, she was happy to curl up in the chair and just flip the pages of an old picture book created with love just for her.

The events of the day had taken their toll on Morgan without her realizing it. As she sat in the window seat looking through the book, she felt her eyes droop.

"Meow."

Morgan jerked awake. She'd dozed off after she quit fighting droopy eyelids, and the sound of a cat meowing at her through the window behind her shoulder had woken her. The light from the library illuminated the immediate area outside of the window, and Morgan could see a beautiful, long-haired tabby kitten. She was sure this was the same cat she'd seen on and off since her arrival to Pearl Island. Slowly getting to her feet so as not to startle the kitten staring intently at her, Morgan moved across to the French doors, ready to invite the kitten to share the library with her. Somehow, she thought the animal belonged to the house, but she wasn't sure. When the kitten marched her way right to the doors, Morgan knew she was right.

"Hello, you sweet thing. You belong here, don't you? But how on earth did you get up here to the second-floor balcony?"

The kitten gave a soft meow as if in answer and rubbed herself against Morgan's ankles in greeting. Deciding she was friendly, Morgan bent down and picked the kitten up, cuddling her as she scratched her behind the ears. The kitten lifted a paw to place it gently against her cheek, and Morgan noticed how large the paw was. Looking at the kitten's front paws closer, she saw the extra "thumb" on each foot. The kitten was a polydactyl cat.

Morgan looked back out the door and saw the large live oak outside the library's window. She had found the route the kitten had taken to reach the second floor. Reaching for the door handle to close the French door, she noticed the mist was beginning again.

"You just keep showing up out of the mist, don't you? Bet you're hungry; let's see if we can find you something to eat."

Still holding the cat, Morgan felt through the thick fur around her neck, hoping for a collar that would identify the kitten, but she found nothing. The kitten squirmed in her arms, so she put her down and followed the kitten as she led the way to the kitchen. It was clear the cat knew her way around the house, and Morgan was happy to find a little companionship thrust upon her through the mist.

She found some food and put it down on the floor for her guest, who quickly gobbled it up. Morgan smiled as the kitten finished and daintily licked her paws to clean her face and long whiskers.

"So, my little friend, what am I going to call you?" Morgan asked out loud as she looked out the window. Then she looked back down at the kitten as inspiration hit her. "How about Misty?"

The kitten looked up at her and meowed as if agreeing. Smiling down at the feline, Morgan snapped her fingers and called her.

"Well then, Misty, come upstairs with me. I have a feeling you're the type of cat who will curl up in bed and claim it for yourself."

The kitten looked at her as if she completely understood every word Morgan said. She swished her tail, walked out of the kitchen and headed right for the stairs to the upper bedrooms.

"Yep, you definitely belong here, Misty."

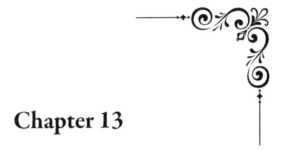

Chapter 13

M organ took a quick shower, drained by the day's events. She had every intention of curling up with another book she had brought along with her. When she came out of the adjoining bathroom, she glanced down at her feet, trying to decide if she wanted to put slippers on to walk out on the widow's walk. Deciding not to, she grabbed the one indulgence she treated herself to. It was a secret indulgence, one that most people would not expect from her. She loved beautiful nightgowns with matching coats, and the one she had on tonight was a simple gown, shimmery blue, full and flowing.

She picked up her book and opened the doors to the widow's walk, letting the fresh air blow through into her room. The night air was crisp and refreshing, and she breathed in deeply the smell of the sea. Taking a step out onto the walkway, Morgan looked at the ocean, seeing the moon shimmer on the waves. Without fear or hesitation, she walked to the railing, looking out over the shoreline. The wind grabbed her nightgown, causing it to billow out behind her, giving her an almost ghostly appearance.

Morgan reached up to push her windblown hair out of her face and frowned. The blue streak of hair color that she playfully had applied to her hair a few weeks ago was still there and showed no signs of diminishing. It was supposed to have been a temporary rinse that comes out after one or two washings. But instead, the color seemed to be intensifying, and it was definitely not coming out. Even with a few weeks' worth of growth on her hair, her roots were still blue. Morgan had noticed when she looked in the mirror after her shower that the original color she had applied was spreading into different shades, and she wondered what in the world was going on. Thankfully it was only a strip on either side of her face, rather than her whole head—how would she ever explain that? Then, defiantly, she shrugged her shoulders. She didn't have to explain her choices to anyone.

"I'm a grown woman, in charge of my own life. And if I feel like having a little bit of blue in my hair, who's around to question me?"

She frowned a bit at that last thought. She was on her own now; there was no one around to question her, and no one to be there for her. Her shoulders sagged at this realization. She'd counted so much on being able to be with her Aunt Meredith to catch up on family life and, yes, to put down some roots.

Standing there, looking over the railing, she began to hear a sound she was becoming familiar with. It was the same six notes that the doorbell had rung. The same six notes that had startled her when Gabriel had first appeared in the mist earlier in the day. The music was haunting as he continued to play, and she found herself leaning over the railing, trying to find him. But the mist had deepened around the house, and she could only hear the sound of his violin. She couldn't see him. Then just as the song started to wind down, Morgan saw a figure walk along the shore through the swirling mist. She took a step back away from the railing, not wanting anybody to see her.

"You can trust him."

Morgan whirled around, looking to see who had spoken, but there was nobody on the deck with her. But she knew the voice, and she knew she had heard the words.

"Aunt Meredith?"

The wind blew a bit harder, and Morgan turned to take another step back towards the bench. She was shocked to see the figure of Meredith Seaver sitting on the bench, the kitten curled up by her side.

"It's okay, Morgan, don't be afraid." Meredith held her hand out for Morgan. After a moment of hesitation, Morgan gingerly sat on the bench, but not too close to the ghostly figure.

"Oh, my dear. Your arrival is certainly not what you expected. And I'm so sorry about that. But things are quickly getting out of control, and you are going to need to take steps to get it back under control. I can't stay long; my powers aren't strong enough. But I can tell you this much. You must find the ring. And when you do, don't take it off. Then my powers will be stronger, and together we will be able to defeat our foes."

As Meredith talked, she began to shimmer and fade.

"Wait! What's going on? What foes? Who killed you?" Morgan hastily cried out, hoping to get at least one answer before she lost her aunt again.

"You'll have to find the answers for yourself. You have friends in town who will help, and of course, there are always answers in the library."

Meredith's voice faded as she slowly disappeared, her last words coming from the air where she had sat.

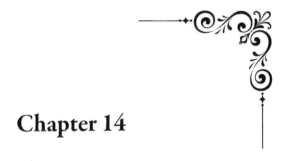

Chapter 14

Morgan woke the next morning to see the sun filtering through the window's lace curtains, promising another beautiful Florida day. She looked around the room, smiling as the memories from her youth came flooding back. Her Aunt Meredith would never change her room, letting Morgan make the changes herself during her visits. There was comfort in those memories, most of her aunt, but a few vague ones of her mother.

She stretched her feet out until they hit something solid. A meow in protest reached her ears, and the memories of the day before came back. It had not been the day she expected, from her arrival to Pearl island, to the discovery of her aunt's death, to the conversation last night with the ghost of her aunt.

The thought of her conversation with Meredith the night before jolted her out of bed. She threw the covers out of her way, partially burying the kitten in the fabric's soft depths. This time her meow was stronger and protesting. Morgan reached down and unburied the kitten, tickling her softly under her chin. The kitten was tangible proof that the events of yesterday had been real.

Determined to get things done today, something that her aunt had hinted would need to happen to provide answers, Morgan placed Misty back on the bed and headed for the bathroom.

Twenty minutes later, the two of them were in the kitchen. Misty was gobbling up the food Morgan put out for her, and Morgan was studying the refrigerator contents, trying to figure out what she wanted for breakfast. Her aunt's kitchen was well stocked, but nothing appealed to Morgan. After yesterday she needed some comfort food, and she knew just the place for it: the pastry shop. The pastry shop was somewhere she and Meredith had spent many mornings catching up on gossip and enjoying the best pastry she'd ever had. Shutting the refrigerator door firmly, Morgan turned and looked down at the contented kitten washing her paws.

"Okay, Misty. I will have to get out there and find out what's going on here on the island sometime. I may as well do it now." Morgan smiled to herself. Talking out loud to the kitten was getting to be a habit.

Grabbing some money out of her purse, Morgan's destination was the storage shed where she knew her aunt stored the bicycles. Golf carts, walking, and bicycling were the main modes of transportation on the island. Pearl Island was too small to accommodate a lot of vehicle traffic, and Morgan remembered that the residents prided themselves on not using their cars. It was mostly the tourists coming onto the island that populated streets. And once they determined there was no place to see or go on the island, they headed back to the beach and parked their cars.

Morgan opened the door to the shed and found the bike she always used when she visited, pleased to see that Meredith had kept it in good repair, as if she had been anticipating the next time Morgan would arrive.

Putting the kickstand down to hold the bike in place, Morgan turned to lock the shed back up. Finished, she turned back to get on the bike and was surprised at the sight in front of her. Misty had jumped into the basket attached to the bike and was staring at her as if waiting to see how Morgan would react.

"And where do you think you're going? You act like this is something you often do, Misty."

The kitten merely yawned at Morgan and turning around in the basket. She found a comfortable spot and curled up, ready to take a midmorning nap. Morgan smiled at the kitten's antics and decided not to disturb her. It was apparent she was used to riding in the basket and to be honest, she enjoyed the kitten's company. It would be nice to have a friend with her because she had no idea what kind of reception she would get when she made it into town.

To make it to the pastry shop, Morgan had to pass by the pizza shop, which she remembered always being full, from lunchtime until closing time, both residents and tourists enjoying the only restaurant on the island. The pastry shop handled the morning business until the pizzeria opened, and it seemed to work out for both eateries. She pedaled past the other buildings that made up the business section of town. On one corner were the post office and town offices, and opposite that was the only church in town that most of the residents called their own. There was a small trinket shop and a convenience store closer to the beach geared more towards the tourists. The only other public building was a small museum in which Morgan remembered having souvenirs from the sea along with historical memorabilia of the island on display for tourists and residents to look at. There was a small one-room gift shop attached to the museum filled with nautical knickknacks and beautiful handmade jewelry.

Morgan arrived at the pastry shop and put her bike into one of the bike racks in front of the building. She picked one in the shade so that the kitten could continue her nap. Morgan had no idea if she would stay in the basket or not, but she felt she should try to make her comfortable.

When Morgan opened the doors to the pastry shop, the smells assaulted her, making her stomach grumble and protest. The sweet aroma of Danish mixed with strong coffee was just what she remembered. She also remembered that this was the central spot for the morning gossip, and as she walked across the lobby to place her order, she could hear the gossip now gear up. She had expected this, but she didn't like it; she hated being the center of attention. As she listened to the whispers behind her back, she knew it wasn't all good attention.

"That's Meredith's niece."

"I hear she's come to live at the Seaver house. I wonder if she'll stay this time?"

"Poor girl, she's the one who found her aunt's body."

"Sirena swears she is the one who killed Meredith."

When Morgan heard the last whisper, she almost turned and walked out. But then the years of training from her aunt kicked in. The years of standing firm and being proud of yourself regardless of what went on around you. Straightening her shoulders, she walked to the counter and placed her order.

"There you go, miss." The girl behind the counter pushed her order on a tray towards her.

Morgan hesitated, ready to ask for a to-go bag. But the girl turned away from her, and she lost the opportunity. Picking up the tray, she turned and walked to an empty table near the window. Looking around, she realized that not all the whispers were unfriendly. She exchanged smiles with a couple sitting at the table next to her as she sat down.

"I'm glad you decided to stay."

Morgan was looking out the window when she heard the voice and looked up to see two women standing next to her. They were both dressed in shorts and tank tops, flip-flops on their feet. It took a moment for Morgan to recognize the woman who spoke to her. With her casual dress and long hair hanging down her back, Morgan didn't immediately recognize Jenny without her uniform.

"You don't mind if we join you, do you? This is my sister, Kathy."

Without waiting for Morgan's answer, Jenny pulled out a chair and sat down while motioning for her sister to join her. As Morgan looked up to the woman, she could see the family resemblance, and she smiled at Jenny, grateful to find a friend.

"Don't forget, Morgan, it's a small town, and there will be gossip. But anybody who's been here long enough knows how much you and Meredith meant to each other. It's hard not to see that there's no way you could have killed your aunt, and as soon as the gossip dies down, everyone else will realize it too. And that will give us a chance to find the real killer."

"Are you any closer to finding the killer?" Morgan interjected. "Have you found any evidence?"

Jenny smiled reassuringly at Morgan "We're handling it. I promise we will find your aunt's killer," she said, and then changed the subject. "So, how was your first night in the Seaver house?"

How did Morgan answer that? Did she dare tell the officer about her ghostly visit? But before she said anything, Kathy pointed out the window at something. Morgan and Jenny followed her fingers, pointing towards the bicycles, and they burst out laughing when they saw Misty's head looking over the rim of the basket.

"I see you found that stray kitten. I know Meredith had been putting food out for her, but she hadn't made friends with it yet. It looks like you succeeded," Kathy said.

"I think it's more she found me. And claimed me. She's a sweet thing. I've named her Misty."

The talk turned more general, and soon the three women were laughing and getting to know each other. It seemed as if Jenny had signaled to the others in the building, and quite a few people stopped by to introduce themselves as they finished their pastries and prepared to leave.

Morgan wanted to ask Jenny again if they had made any progress on finding her aunt's killer, but she didn't want to disrupt the pleasantness of the pastry shop with the talk of death. Right now, she was being accepted, and she didn't want to remind the shop's patrons about the murder.

They sat and talked for about a half-hour, and then finally, it was time to leave. After cleaning off the table, the three walked to the front door. Kathy hurried over to the bike to say hello to Misty. Jenny took that opportunity to give a bit of advice to Morgan.

"Strange things happen on the island, things that can't always be explained. Keep an open mind. You will have a lot of questions. You might find some answers over at the museum."

Walking over to her sister, Jenny pried her away from the kitten. Laughing, the two sisters waved to Morgan and headed in the opposite direction of the beach towards the residential area of Pearl Island.

Chapter 15

M organ studied the old building in front of her, admiring the simple architecture. There was nothing fancy in the design of the building. It was sturdy and had withstood time and the ravages of weather along the shore. It had been years since Morgan had been inside the museum. Not since she was a child, most likely, because her memories were of looking into the showpieces rather than looking down on them, which would indicate that she was a child at the time.

Morgan had ridden her bike over to the museum, rather than leaving her bike at the pastry shop. It was a short distance, and she could have easily walked it, but she knew how valuable those spots were for other bikers to park and use while they were in the shop. Misty had been content to go for the short ride, but now she stood at Morgan's feet, playing a game of wrapping herself around Morgan's ankles.

"Keep it up, little one, and you're gonna trip me," she admonished the kitten. Misty merely swished her tail a bit harder before walking to the front door of the building.

"What makes you think they would let a cat in the museum?" Morgan laughed at Misty.

The front door to the museum opened, and before Morgan could stop her, the kitten rushed inside. The woman staring back at Morgan looked slightly amused as Morgan apologized for the cat's intrusion.

"There's no sense apologizing for a cat," the woman said. "They do what they want when they want. Besides, this cat is here often. She does no harm, so I don't see any reason to shoo her out. But I would like to welcome you in. You're Meredith's niece, aren't you? It's easy to see the family resemblance." Holding the door open a little wider, the woman motioned for Morgan to enter. "I'm Erwinia Colbright. Come in, I think you'll find there's quite a bit of interest in here for you. By the way, I was a good friend of your aunt's, and I'm so sorry for her loss."

Morgan accepted the condolences as she walked into the building, her eyes adjusting to the dimmer light. She looked around her in astonishment. How could one person get so much in a small room and make it seem so organized? She had an idea that it was the woman in front of her who had managed this feat. Then something she had said clicked with Morgan.

"Colbright? Are you any relation to Jenny and Kathy?"

"Yes, they're my granddaughters, as different as night and day. Jenny, she's an upstanding police officer, as you know, and Kathy is more like a gypsy flitting from one spot to another. It's always nice when she comes back to Pearl Island to stay for a while. You caught her on one of her rare visits."

"I'm pleased to meet you, Erwinia. Your granddaughters have both made me feel welcome to Pearl Island."

"Oh, please call me Winnie. Your aunt always did."

"Then, in that case, I'm happy to call you Winnie. Now, can you give me a tour? I bet there's a story behind every piece and showcase."

"There most certainly is, and a fair amount of them revolve around the Seaver family," a male voice said from the doorway.

Both women turned and instantly smiled when they saw Dylan. Misty had seen the man before the two women had heard him, and she was nestled in his arms as he scratched her ears.

"Good morning, Dylan." Winnie greeted him with a sad smile, and Morgan realized that the two of them were grieving the loss of her aunt, just as she was. The three of them had been close in age and formed a friendship that had lasted for years.

Dylan hugged each of the women, and the moment passed. Winnie made a big show of gathering a pile of papers that lay on one of the display cases and walked to a small desk hidden in a corner.

"Dylan, you know as much about the stuff in here as I do. Why don't you give Morgan the five-cent tour? I need to answer these letters."

"Winnie, you know plenty, don't sell yourself short," he protested.

"Yes, I do. But I think you have a closer tie to this matter than I do. My family has only been a recorder of events. Whereas yours..." The woman gave him a knowing look as her words trailed off.

Dylan returned her look, and then he nodded in agreement. Without another word, Winnie went to her desk and made herself busy. Turning back to Morgan, Dylan spread his arms wide.

"Where would you like to start? Everything ties together here; everything has a story."

Morgan looked around her with interest. Winnie had organized things in groups, and it was easy to see that some were more educational and others more of a personal nature. She bypassed the display of nautical-themed items, glanced briefly at the display case of beautiful old jewelry. She noticed that a large portion of them contained pearls.

"Pearls are always in abundance on Pearl Island." Winnie laughed at her own pun before adding a little tidbit of interest. "Legend has it that pearls come from the teardrops of mermaids."

Morgan looked in the desk's direction to find Winnie watching their every move. She seemed serious about her statement and the attempt at a little joke. Morgan had been ready to say something else, but the words died in her throat. She had a feeling that Winnie believed in that legend. Saying nothing, Morgan continued on to the next display case. This was more interesting to her.

Carefully on display under the glass were beautiful old books, and Morgan was sure she had seen similar ones in her aunt's library. Mixed in with the books were small figurines of mermaids and dolphins. It made for a whimsical display, and Morgan couldn't help but smile.

"These books are gorgeous," Morgan said. "And they appear to be in excellent condition. You have done a good job preserving them, Winnie."

"Preserving the legends of Pearl Island is a task my family has handled for many years." The voice from the desk was prideful and serious.

"Yes, Pearl Island has a lot to be thankful for when it comes to the Colbright family," Dylan said. "They have preserved our history for as long as anybody can remember. And you're right, Morgan, many of these same books are in your library. Meredith donated a few of them for the display here in the museum."

Morgan looked between the two of them, sensing an undertone. But she couldn't put her finger on it, so she asked the first question that came to mind.

"Winnie, does that mean that one of your granddaughters will take over the museum someday?"

"Yes, I'm proud to say that Jenny has taken an interest and works here most weekends when she's off duty. She has a love for history as most first daughters in our family have."

The older woman answered her question, and then pointedly took a more avid look at what was going on at her desk. She was turning the questions over to Dylan to answer. Morgan hid a smile, wondering how long it would be before the older woman interrupted with another piece of information.

Morgan and Dylan continued looking at the different display pieces. They were almost finished when her eyes locked onto a beautiful painting. Without a word, she walked over to stand in front of it, mesmerized by its beauty and something else. It was almost as if the artwork was trying to tell her something.

The painting had captured a stormy night along the beach. Morgan could feel the anger and danger illuminating from the artist's work. On the shore stood a man looking out to sea, his arms wide, mist swirling around his feet. To the right and the left of the man, Morgan saw two female mermaids. One was crying, and the other seemed to be in a rage. Morgan could almost feel the fury. As she looked closely at the crying mermaid, she saw the pearls floating on the surrounding water, and remembered what Winnie had told her moments before. It was a haunting scene, and it shook Morgan to her very core.

"Who painted this?" Morgan whispered, almost afraid to hear the answer.

"It was one of your ancestors, one of the very first Seavers on Pearl Island." Dylan answered her in a reverent tone.

"This painting almost feels real, it's so haunting, so emotional." Morgan shook her shoulders as if to rid herself of the power the painting had over her.

The other two didn't answer, and Morgan moved away from the art, glancing over her shoulders a final time. From this angle, she could see more details. Each of the mermaids had a gathering of sea animals and other mermaids behind them as if they had formed an army. The one group of mermaids was beautiful until you looked closer at them, and they swam behind the furious mermaid in the foreground. The sea animals were hard to make out but gave the feeling of danger. Behind the mermaid who cried, Morgan could see dolphins and other mermaids who looked like their leader. Morgan was in awe of the talent of the artist who had painted the picture.

The sound of something hitting the floor broke the spell. Morgan and the others turned to look at Misty standing on one counter, her tail swishing. It only took a second to realize she had pushed off a stack of brochures sitting on the countertop. Morgan could almost swear the cat was pleased with herself, and she quickly scolded the feline.

"I bet you did that on purpose, didn't you? What's the matter, not getting enough attention?" Bending over, she quickly scooped up the pamphlets and placed them back on the counter. She held one in her hands and looked over at Winnie, asking if she could take it with her.

"That's what they're there for. But I think you'll find more answers in Meredith's library then in that brochure. You go back and look; you'll find the meaning behind that picture. And take that silly cat home, before she gets into more trouble."

Morgan assured the woman that she would take the cat and skedaddle, but before she did, she looked over at Dylan and thanked him for spending the time with her.

"You helped me see some interesting things here, Dylan. I don't know why but when I'm around you, I feel comfortable, almost safe. And I'm sure my aunt Meredith did too." She reached over and squeezed his hand. "I know you're missing her more than I ever could. The two of you had a special bond, and I thank you for always being there for her." Then Morgan scooped up the cat and opened the door to leave.

As she opened the door, she saw the figure of a woman rushing away from the front of the building. With her long curls, it was easy to see it was Sirena. But it wasn't until Morgan looked around her that she realized just how much the other woman disliked her. There in front of her was her bike, laying on its side, the basket tore apart, two flat tires, and a screwdriver driven into the chain of the bike.

"What the heck?" Morgan called out to the retreating woman.

Chapter 16

Morgan turned, ready to run after the girl who was quickly putting distance between them, but before she could take two steps, two strong arms wrapped themselves around her, holding her in place. Frustrated, she squirmed, trying to break free.

"Not now, Morgan. It's not the right time." Dylan's soft voice calmed her anger, bringing her to her senses. She turned to Dylan and Winnie, who would come running at her shout and pointed toward her bike.

"Do you see what Sirena did? Just look at the bike! What did I ever do to her?"

Dylan and Winnie exchanged looks before the older woman calmed her down.

"It's just a bike, Morgan. We'll call Jenny and tell her what happened; make an official police report. It's best to do this right away. Don't forget Sirena has accused you of murder so if you go chasing after her—"

"Winnie's right. Let the law handle the vandalism. Besides, take a good look at the damage. Does that look like the work of somebody you want to confront?"

Morgan thought about Dylan's words as she looked down at her bike and shuddered. It was the screwdriver sticking out of the chain that convinced her they were both right. There was a lot of anger and maliciousness in the thrust of that screwdriver. And Morgan felt relief; it was the bike that had felt the brunt of the rage and not her.

Seeing that she had accepted their words, Winnie went back into the shop and called her granddaughter. Twenty minutes later, a report had been made. But because Morgan had only seen the backside of the woman running away, she couldn't positively identify Sirena. Jenny promised to question the accused woman, but she warned Morgan that without proof it was just a he-said-she-said situation.

As they were wrapping up, Jenny got another call and had to leave. Winnie returned into the museum to finish her paperwork, and Morgan stood looking down at the bike. Her anger turned to frustration.

"Come on, Morgan, we'll throw the bike in the back of my car, and I'll get it home for you," Dylan said. "The bike needs repair work, but at least you have another one to ride. I know Meredith always kept hers in good shape." He wrapped his arms around her shoulders, giving her a squeeze of encouragement.

This encouragement worked. Morgan stood straighter and gave a small stamp of her foot. "I don't know what Sirena has against me, but I'm not letting her stop me from making myself part of the community. This is my home now. In truth, it always has been my home. I've just been absent, but that has come to an end. And she's just going to have to get used to it."

"That's the spirit."

"You know what, Dylan? It's not that far. I'd rather carry the bike home. As a show of defiance."

Dylan laughed out loud. "You are so much like your aunt. Okay, if that's the way you want to do it. You grab one end, I'll grab the other."

"You don't need to help me with it."

"Yes, I do." Dylan's answer was simple, and his tone didn't allow for any argument.

Walking over to the bike, he picked up the back end and grinned at her. Now smiling and feeling rather foolish, Morgan walked over and grabbed the other end. They proceeded down the main street of the island towards the Seaver house. By the time they had reached the house, they were laughing and talking, making a bad situation into an opportunity to get to know each other better. A couple of people had stopped them along the way, showing sympathy for what had happened. Whether or not Morgan knew it, she was gaining respect within the community, and sides were being formed.

"CAN IT BE SAVED?"

Morgan looked at the bike leaning up against the storage shed wall then looked over at Dylan.

"Of course, it can. I like to work on bikes. I'll take it on as my personal task." Dylan rubbed his hands together as if he was a child eagerly anticipating a gift.

"You don't have to do that, Dylan. If you think we can salvage the bike, I can have it taken to a bike shop and fixed."

"Nonsense, it will give me something to do."

But Morgan heard something more in his tone, and she had a feeling he was using the bike as an excuse to keep an eye on her. At this point, she didn't mind. On the walk home, she caught a few glares from people she didn't even know, and it made her uncomfortable. She always had thought she was likable and had never had a problem making friends, but for some reason, there were those on Pearl Island who seemed to take an instant dislike to her, and she couldn't explain it.

"Well, if you're sure?" She watched him nod his head and returned the smile he gave her. "How about a cold drink first?"

Dylan wiped the dirt from the bike tires on the back of his pants and agreed to her suggestion. They walked to the front door, and before Morgan even had the door all the way open, Misty disappeared inside.

"Why do I think she's up to something?" Morgan asked out loud.

She suggested they take a seat on the front porch, and when Dylan agreed, she went into the kitchen to grab some cold drinks and some cookies she'd seen. She remembered Dylan had a sweet tooth. They spent a pleasant half an hour, talking about anything but the bike. Morgan asked questions about some things she'd seen in the museum, and Dylan was happy to explain more history surrounding the island. But when she asked about the painting, he shook his head.

"You will have to find the answers about that on your own."

"Why is everybody so mysterious about things around here?"

"Because some things are just best discovered by yourself. Now I need to get moving, and I believe you wanted to go up into the library and start searching."

Getting to his feet, Dylan handed her his glass and walked down the stairs and gave his parting reminder.

"And keep an eye out for that ring."

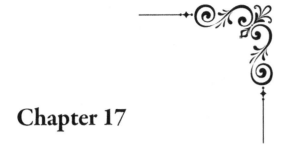

Chapter 17

Morgan stood in the center of the library, looking around. There were so many books, it was almost overwhelming. Misty had followed her up the stairs and now stood at her ankles, doing her little dance of weaving between her legs, rubbing against her, and tickling Morgan's calves with her tail. Bending down, Morgan picked up the feline and walked over to the window seat.

"So, where do I start?"

Misty gave a soft meow, as if in answer, and then butted her head gently against Morgan's chin. Morgan chuckled and then looked down on the bench and saw the brochure she had picked up from the museum. As she absentmindedly ran one hand down Misty's smooth fur, she used the other to flip open the catalog. She glanced at the contents and then looked back up at the rows of books.

"Well, Misty, this brochure talks about the history of Pearl Island. It's clear my family has played a huge role in the island's development. Heck, this says the founding father of the island was a Seaver." Misty didn't bother to answer. Instead, she moved from Morgan's lap to the bench, sitting on top of the brochure in the process.

"Oh, you're a lot of help. But maybe you're right; Winnie said the answer was in the past. Aunt Meredith and I never talked much about the past. We were always too busy trying to catch up on the here and now to worry about what had already taken place years ago. So, I'll start with the oldest books."

When Morgan got up, her bracelet snagged on one of the pillows lining the window. She took a moment to take the bracelet off and then set it on the desk as she walked by it. She headed for a section of shelves that seemed to hold the oldest books in the room.

As Morgan looked at the books, she realized they were part of the same collection held within glass cases at the museum. This was an excellent place to start. Reaching out, she grabbed one off the shelf and opened it up to find it was a personal journal. It only took a moment to realize the journals were from the early Seavers who had settled the island.

The binding and spine were fragile, and the pages yellowed, causing Morgan to treat the book with care. She made a mental note to herself that this needed to be one of her first priorities, to catalog and repair the library's books.

It didn't take long for Morgan to get lost in the words on the page. She always loved to read, but this was different. This was personal; it was her history, and hopefully, somewhere in the pages, she would find the answers to the whispers she'd heard since she got to the island.

A woman with flowing handwriting wrote the first few books that she looked at. The script was so elaborate, there were times it was hard for Morgan to read the words, but she'd run across this style of writing many times in the past when preserving books from this era. Once she got used to the style, it was easier to read, and she found herself fascinated by the words the woman had written about the island life. In her experience, most journals written in this time were a daily account of what went on with the family. But this Seaver enjoyed including family antics and her personal feelings, and it didn't take long for Morgan to lose herself in the woman's words.

"Listen to this, Misty. She talks about the strange mist that appears on the island. Oh, and here she hints about mermaids." Morgan gave a short laugh and looked up, expecting to see Misty curled up in the window seat where she had left her. But the kitten had made her way to the desk, and Morgan watched, astonished as the cat used her mouth to pick up the bracelet Morgan had set there.

"Misty. What are you doing? Put that down."

The kitten looked up, startled, and met Morgan's glance. Morgan swore there was a devious twinkle in her eye and not one ounce of guilt. With a swish of her tail, the kitten jumped from the desk, hurrying out of the room, Morgan's bracelet still in her mouth.

"Misty! Wait."

Morgan put the book carefully down and then rushed after the kitten to retrieve her bracelet. But Misty had a head start, and Morgan didn't find her right away. She searched a couple of rooms and then finally saw the cat as she turned the corner in the hallway on her way up the stairs.

Morgan followed her, surprised when she bypassed the bedrooms and went to a door at the end of the hallway. The kitten pushed on the door, and slowly, it opened. She squeezed her way inside. Morgan couldn't remember what was in this room.

Pushing open the door, Morgan followed the cat into the room. Meredith had used it as a storage workroom of sorts. The room was deceptively large, and it stored a few pieces of discarded furniture, boxes marked personal, and a rack filled with old vintage clothing. But Morgan wasn't interested in that; she was more interested in getting what had been stolen from her. The thief was standing in the middle of the room, daring her to come and take what was hers.

"Misty, you little troublemaker, give that back to me."

The kitten ignored Morgan and walked to the corner behind a few boxes, the bracelet dangling from her mouth. Sighing with frustration, Morgan pushed the boxes out of her way in her attempts to get to the kitten. When she finally reached the kitten in the corner, she was astonished to see the treasures Misty had accumulated. How long she'd been stealing, Morgan had no idea, but she had quite the collection.

"Oh, you've been busy, haven't you? How long have you been doing this? Let me in there, and let's see what you've got stashed."

Morgan dropped to her knees so she could better examine Misty's stash. There was a range of items, and most of them seemed to be shiny things that had caught the kitten's eye. Morgan was astonished as she sifted through the items on the floor.

"How in the world did you carry this up here?" she asked the kitten, holding up a pickle fork she remembered her aunt having in her silver set.

Giggling, Morgan held up the items one by one, teasing the kitten as she did. Small pieces of jewelry similar to her bracelet, a pair of eyeglasses that had a gold chain attached to them, glittering bookmarks, small pieces of crystal that she remembered her aunt using in making jewelry, were just a few of the treasures.

"Well, you have good taste," Morgan teased the kitten, and she held up a pretty earring that had no match. With her other hand, she moved two bookmarks, their tassels made from a glittery yarn.

Her hand froze as she moved the last bookmark, and she gasped. Underneath the markers was a ring.

Morgan knew instinctively this was the ring Meredith had instructed her to find. With hands that shook just a little, she reached out and picked up the ring.

"I don't know if I should scold you or hug you."

The kitten came and sat on her lap while Morgan looked at the ring. She had a feeling that Misty's theft of the ring had protected it from the intruder who had searched Meredith's office.

Morgan got to her feet and walked over to a small window, wishing to get a better look at the ring. At first glance, it was simple in design, but as she looked harder, she could see it was old. It was more than old; it was ancient, and the design on the band was an intricate play of dolphins and mermaids. The top of the ring where you would typically find a stone or gem was a beautiful gold shell. The design on the band became raised as it neared the shell, and on either side of the shell was a mermaid, her hands lifted as if holding the shell in place. There was a tiny hinge on the back of the shell, but when Morgan tried to open it, it wouldn't budge. She didn't want to press any harder for fear of breaking the hinge.

Morgan's hands seemed to have a mind of their own, and without her even realizing what she was doing, she slid the ring on her finger. It was a perfect fit. She stood admiring it for a moment, and then her mouth opened in astonishment as she watched the shell slowly open.

Sitting in the now open-shell was the most perfect pearl Morgan had ever seen. Not only was it perfect in shape, but the color was amazing. It wasn't pure white or black or pink or blue. The gem was none of the standard colors found in a jewelry store. No, this pearl was almost iridescent, a mixture of all colors, along with gold flecks that seemed to radiate from the pearl.

"Oh, my...."

Morgan was at a loss for words. She stood staring at the ring on her finger, mesmerized by the colors of the sea gem. Looking at the ring, she felt calmer and almost had a sense of inner strength. She closed her eyes for a moment, letting the feelings engulf her. When she opened her eyes, she was astonished to see the pearl was no longer visible; the shell had closed back up. Morgan tried with her fingernail to open it again, but it wouldn't budge. Had she just imagined the whole thing?

"Meow."

Morgan looked down at the cat and gave a small laugh. The kitten had brought her bracelet back to her and was standing at her feet. Reaching down, Morgan picked up the kitten and cuddled Misty, taking the bracelet gently from her mouth and slipping it into her pocket.

"Thank you, Misty," Morgan said, but she wasn't sure which piece of jewelry she was thanking her for, the bracelet she had stolen or the ring she had hidden.

VICTORIA LK WILLIAMS

Chapter 18

Morgan spent the rest of the day running between the library and the front door. Friends of her Aunt Meredith's had come calling. Most came with gifts of casseroles or baked goods; all came expressing their deep sorrow for the passing of a good friend.

Dylan and Gabriel had come together, passing on the news that everything was set for the memorial service that Meredith had pre-planned; it would be the next morning. When they told her the service would not be at the church but down on the beach near the outcropping of rocks, Morgan wasn't surprised. That was her aunt's special place, and it was only fitting that her friends and family say goodbye to her there.

She discovered more secrets within the journals, but nothing that answered the questions she was constantly asking herself. She quickly learned as she went through the journals that the Seaver family had not only been founding fathers of the island community, they'd also been leaders. Almost protectors of the community. They held high positions in the small local government and gave up their own possessions to help the township when it ran into troubles. They organized cleanups after storms that threatened the coast. It surprised Morgan to find out that a hurricane had never made a direct hit on the island even though it was right in the pathway of most of the seasonal storms. It was as if the island had some special protection.

It was evening by the time the last of her visitors left, and Morgan was exhausted. She usually led a solitary life and being around this many people drained her. She was coming to grips with the fact that her aunt was no longer with her and that she was the last Seaver on the island. She knew in her heart that she was meant to be there, and she would stay. She could conduct her business from the beach house. There was a room down by the library that she would turn into her workshop, and she'd already started setting up her equipment.

Morgan heated one of the small casseroles that Meredith's friends had left her for dinner. After cleaning up, she grabbed a slice of chocolate cake that had also been delivered and made a carafe of coffee, placing them on the tray along with her cup.

Morgan carried the tray up to her room. After opening the doors to the widow's walk, she called Misty and walked outside, setting the tray on a small table. She thought about bringing another journal with her, but she was too tired. A sweet treat and the cleansing air of the sea was what she needed right now.

"You found the ring."

Morgan looked to the railing, not surprised to see her aunt standing there, her figure slightly translucent, shimmering in the wind.

"Yes, thanks to Misty."

"That's a good name for her. I'm glad she's keeping you company. Now that you're wearing the ring, Morgan, it will set things in motion. You must be strong, but don't be afraid to rely on those who have your best interest at heart."

Before Morgan could answer her, Meredith disappeared. Morgan got to her feet and walked over to the railing where her aunt had just a moment before appeared. There was a mist along the shore. It seemed to encircle the house as if it was a cloak of protection. Through the mist, Morgan faintly heard a violin playing a now-familiar tune.

THE NEXT MORNING WAS glorious. The sun shone, the breeze was gentle, and the ocean calm. Morgan knew that Gabriel and Dylan would come to get her shortly but she wanted a moment to herself first. Slipping out into the courtyard, she followed the path to the garden and walked until she came to the gate. She punched in the code Dylan had given her and entered the peacock's realm. The birds didn't seem at all upset to have her walk with them, and almost seemed to lead her to a beautiful structure she hadn't noticed before. It appeared her Aunt Meredith had not only welcomed the peacocks, but she'd built a beautiful open aviary for them to roost at night safely, too. Walking to the aviary, Morgan found a bin filled with hand-pruned seed heads. Opening the lid, the peacocks gathered around her, and Morgan guessed this was a treat. Reaching inside, she selected a few seedpods and gently placing them on the ground, not sure how the peacocks would react to her. The birds waited for a moment and then almost politely came forward, and each took the seed head and retreated. Morgan felt like they had established a rapport, and she sighed, happy with one small accomplishment this morning. Realizing time was passing, she left the area and went back to the house and found Gabriel and Dylan waiting for her.

Together the three of them walked down to the beach where friends had gathered. Dylan read a prepared speech that Meredith had given him. She thanked those who had come for their years of friendship and love, asking that they look after Morgan in her absence. As Dylan finished, Gabriel picked up his violin and played the same melody. Slowly the guests left, offering condolences to Morgan on their way. When most of them had left, Morgan looked up to see a stunning woman with long dark hair making her way towards her.

Instinctively Morgan stiffened her back, but she didn't take a step away. The others who were left became silent. Even Gabriel stopped playing.

"I'm Cora Sharp. I knew your aunt for many years." The woman stood in front of Morgan, holding out her hand.

Morgan couldn't help but notice she didn't say she was a friend of her aunt's or offer any condolences. She was merely introducing herself. Morgan felt like she was being challenged, and she held out her hand, accepting the other woman's handshake. She was right; she was being challenged. Morgan didn't flinch as the woman's hands closed tightly over hers, squeezing as hard as she could. Suddenly the woman stopped and looked down at Morgan's fingers.

"I see you're wearing your aunt's ring. Challenge accepted." With a sneer, the woman turned on her heel and stormed away from the few remaining at the beach.

Astonished, Morgan turned to Dylan for an explanation.

But before he could say anything, Winnie spoke. "That's bold. I can't believe Cora had the nerve to show up here. You watch out for that one, Morgan. She's not to be trusted, and she's not what she seems."

Without another word, the older woman turned and headed back to the dune, taking the same steps Cora had.

"Come on, Kathy, we better stop her before she says something to Cora," Jenny said to her sister and then turned to Morgan, promising to come and see her later. Jenny's departure was like a silent signal for the rest, and they followed up the dunes to return to their homes.

As the mourners walked away, Morgan felt the burn of someone staring at her, and she looked around to see who it was. Her eyes locked with Stanley, and she felt an involuntary shudder run down her back. Next to him was Sirena, dressed in black, as though she was mourning Meredith's death. Stanley continued to stare until Sirena said something to him, and they turned and walked away with the final mourners.

Morgan turned her attention back to those by her side, and she couldn't help but see that Dylan seemed a bit shaken by the confrontation with Cora. He met her glance then, without a word, he walked down towards the water's edge. Morgan made as if to take a step towards him, but Gabriel stopped her.

"Let him be for now. He's lost a great friend."

"Of course, he has. You're right, let's let him have a few moments alone. Come back to the house with me? I have questions, and maybe you can answer them. And the first one is, who is Cora Sharp?"

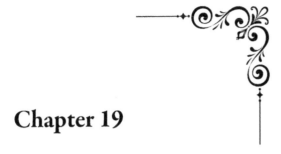

Chapter 19

"So, what's with the violin?"

Morgan and Gabriel were sitting on the front porch while they waited for Dylan to return. Gabriel had been giving Morgan a bit of history about some of the guests who had attended Meredith's memorial service. Her question was out of the blue and took him off guard.

"What do you mean?" he asked.

"You have such talent. It just seems strange that you are so often on the beach playing, instead of giving concerts. To be honest, the first time I heard you, it scared me. Then the second time, you reminded me of the Pied Piper, and I looked to see if there was an entourage around you."

Gabriel laughed at her words, and she smiled back at him.

"I always seem to hear the same melody; do you play anything else?"

Gabriel didn't answer. Instead, he opened the violin case and pulled out the beautifully crafted instrument. With a wicked grin, he quickly started playing a popular Taylor Swift melody.

When he finished, Morgan clapped her hands. "I was right, you're very talented."

She glanced at the violin case and saw some sheet music. She reached down without asking and picked it up. Looking over the page, she found only the instrumental score on the paper, no lyrics. She studied it for a moment and then hummed a few bars.

Gabriel looked at her in surprise before smiling. "You can read music?"

"Yes, I even play the flute. Of course, it's been a few years since I bothered, but I've always been able to read music. It's like a different form of words on the paper. You wouldn't happen to have the score for the melody I keep hearing you play in there, do you?"

Gabriel gave her an odd look and seemed to hesitate. Then he seemed to come to a decision and looked through the paperwork, pulling out the music sheet of the tune he knew so well by heart. Whether or not she realized it, Morgan knew it by heart too. Morgan looked down at the paper in her hands and felt a sense of disappointment.

"I thought for sure there would be beautiful lyrics to go with this melody, but I guess not." Morgan handed the paperwork back to Gabriel, but he motioned for her to look at it again.

"Go ahead and hum the melody. Maybe it will remind you of some lyrics."

Morgan looked at him and saw he was serious. She found she was completely at ease with him, not feeling self-conscious at his request. Clearing her throat, she hummed the first stanza of the music in front of her. The melody was beautiful, and she continued. Reaching the end of the page, she looked up at Gabriel and smiled. He lifted his violin and nodded to her and played the music. Without hesitation, she hummed along with him. She knew the first few stanzas by heart after hearing Gabriel play so many times, but when she stumbled over the rest of the notes, she had to look down at the music. She was astonished at what she saw. Written clearly underneath the musical notes were the lyrics to the melody. Her breath caught in her throat, and she stopped humming. As she hesitated, the words faded.

"Keep going, Morgan," Gabriel softly said.

Morgan hesitated, not sure what was happening, but when she saw that the writing was becoming harder to read, she picked up the music sheet and hummed again, reading the words as she did. Together they finished the music and, without hesitating, played the tune a second time. Now she could read the lyrics entirely. She didn't try to memorize the words, knowing they might disappear, but she could understand the story they told. Morgan looked at Gabriel in bewilderment when he put the violin down across his lap.

"What just happened? How is this even possible?"

"In case you haven't noticed, there are a lot of things unexplained on this island. Things that have laid dormant for years, but now, I think because you're here, they're coming back to the surface. The Seavers always had a reason and a purpose for being on this island. You know that, don't you?"

"Yes, I'm beginning to understand that. But what I don't understand is why am I suddenly becoming part of the island's legacy?"

"Because it is time. Meredith knew this. That's why she encouraged you to return home."

Morgan was silent for a few moments, thinking over what Gabriel had said. The lyrics on the page made sense to her since she had read so much of the journals earlier, and they had told much of the same thing, but she didn't understand at the time when she was reading them.

Sadly, she looked up at Gabriel, almost afraid to ask what was on her mind. "Did my Aunt Meredith know she would die?"

"I think so. She knew there was a force stronger than her that was taking shape and she wasn't able to hold off much longer on her own. That's why she wanted you to return. I don't think she expected to die so suddenly or without helping you understand what was going on."

Dylan's voice came from the bottom of the stairs, and it was he who answered Morgan's question. The two had been so intent with the music they hadn't noticed him walk up the walkway.

"You knew this, Dylan?" Morgan asked.

"Meredith and I talked about it. There wasn't much your aunt and I didn't talk about. And I'm furious with myself that I wasn't there when she was attacked. I should have been able to help her."

By now, Dylan was at the top of the stairs, and Morgan threw down the sheet music and rushed to him, hugging him fiercely.

"You can't blame yourself, Dylan. Aunt Meredith would never tolerate that. I don't understand what's going on, but I know that you and my aunt were soul-mates, and if you'd been able to help her, you would have."

Dylan returned her hug and then led her back over to the couch and sat down next to her. Gabriel sat on her other side, and between the two of them, Morgan felt like she was sandwiched between a protective core.

"There are forces on this island that you cannot underestimate, but you can conquer. When the time is right, you'll know what needs to be done. Until then, you need to keep your guard up. Gabe and I will be here to help you all we can. And there are other families on this island that have always stood firm with the Seavers. You'll soon learn who they are."

Morgan nodded, not understanding what he meant but understanding his tone. Then she smiled at the shortening of Gabriel's name. It seemed to fit him so much better than his regal given name, and she said so. The two men smiled at her in agreement.

"Yeah, Gabriel's rather an ostentatious name. I was going to ask you to call me Gabe, but it looks like my uncle beat me to it." Gabe laughed.

"I asked this when we first got back to the house, but you managed to avoid answering me. Who is Cora? She's part of all this, isn't she?" Getting serious, Morgan looked at the men sitting on either side of her. She stared at Gabe, waiting for an answer.

Before he could answer, Dylan got to his feet. "It's been a long morning. Things are happening faster than I thought they would be. And you are discovering this on your own, not like your aunt would have wanted if she'd had a choice. Why don't we leave you so you can rest?"

"You're avoiding my question, aren't you?"

Gabe reached over and squeezed her hand reassuringly before he scooped up his music sheets and instrument. "You know the answer in your heart," he said. "Think about the music and what it had to say, think about the journals. You'll find your answers, maybe not all at once. But as you find answers, I'll be here to help you understand them."

And with a slight hesitation, Gabe bent over, kissing her forehead before walking down the stairs.

Dylan was not far behind him.

Chapter 20

It had been a few days since Meredith's memorial service. Morgan had spent most of her time reacquainting herself with the family home. Although Meredith hadn't reappeared before Morgan again, there were clear signs that she had been there. A photo album had suddenly appeared on Morgan's bed. Inside she found pictures of herself as a child, a picture she'd forgotten about that included both her mother and her aunt. She curled up with Misty out on the widow's walk and returned to the words in the book time after time, remembering things from her past.

Some jewelry appeared in the desk, and Morgan knew it hadn't been there the last time she had been in Meredith's office. She had gone back to get the other envelopes from the desk drawer, finally looking through the legal documents that gave her possession of the house and all its contents. She was pleased to see there were trusts for different charities on the island that the family had looked after for years. Meredith had even thoughtfully left instructions that the peacock sanctuary was to be left untouched.

Other than the physical evidence that Morgan found, she knew Meredith had been there because there was always the sweet smell of the sea left in the room, a little tangy from salt, fresh, and refreshing.

Morgan had returned to the museum twice to stare at the picture of the mermaids. There was something there that haunted her, and she had to figure out what it was. It was something tangible, something that had just happened in the last few days, but she couldn't put her finger on it.

Using Meredith's bike, she had made her way from one end of the island to the other, getting reacquainted with old favorite places of her youth. Often, she caught up with Kathy or Jenny, either together or separately. The three of them were becoming friends, something Morgan hadn't allowed herself to develop in a long time. She traveled too much with her job to form lasting friendships. She had plenty of acquaintances, some of them close acquaintances, but not real friends.

Dylan showed up every day to check on her, sometimes bringing wildflowers, other times food he thought she might need. Finally, Morgan told him to stop bringing the food; there was plenty at the house, more than she could ever eat before it spoiled. Gabe had dropped by a few times as well, but he seemed to be keeping his distance, as though he was waiting for Morgan to seek him out. But she knew he was there, and she felt protected by both him and Dylan as if they were looking out for her.

Morgan had deliberately kept herself from thinking about what had happened with the sheet music. She put it down to the stress of her aunt's murder, until the third day after the memorial service when she was forced to consider what had happened.

"Misty, have you been at it again?" Morgan had just spent the last half hour searching for a small piece of equipment that she used for her book mending. The cat had walked into what she was now using as a workshop, looking smug.

The cat walked over to her, doing her little dance around her ankles, almost tripping Morgan as she tried to walk towards the workbench she had set up. Reaching out to regain her balance, Morgan's hands sent some paperwork flying to the floor.

"You silly kitten. One of these days, you'll make me break a leg." Frustrated, Morgan righted herself and bent over to gather the papers. But one sheet had gotten underneath a small chair that was in the room's corner. Getting down on her hands and knees, she crawled as close as she could to the legs of the chair and stretched her arms out to grab the piece of paper. Instead, her hand rested on a long, cylindrical object, and she pulled it out, not knowing what to expect.

"Oh, my goodness, I'd forgotten about this. It's been years since I saw it last."

Morgan looked down at the hand-carved recorder, a flute-like musical instrument that she had first learned to play before she graduated to a flute. She had been a child, and she could remember her mother teaching her how to play the instrument. Instinctively, without even thinking about it, she wiped the mouthpiece on her shirt and put the recorder to her mouth and played a few bars. But she quickly stopped when she realized what she was playing. It was the same melody that Gabe seemed to be always playing.

Now she knew why it was so familiar. Her mother had insisted that she learn this piece perfectly, above all other pieces she'd ever played. Morgan remembered the story that both her aunt and her mother had told her while she played the melody. It was the same story she had read in the music a few days earlier on Gabe's music sheets. Sitting back on her bottom, she crossed her legs and closed her eyes. The cat curled up in her lap like she had done something right, and Morgan began to play. She played the entire melody, not missing a note. And as Morgan played, the memory of the voices from the two women she loved most seemed to whisper in her ears. By the time she finished, tears ran down her cheeks. Putting the recorder down next to her, she picked up the cat and hugged her until Misty protested, meowing.

"I remember the story now, Misty. It was a story of love and hate. How much of it is true, who knows? I'm sure some parts are based on truth, but the rest of it has to be fiction." She pulled herself to her feet and, with the cat still in her arms, walked out to sit on the porch looking out to the ocean. The cat seemed content to listen to her voice, and Morgan told the cat the story she had been told as a child.

"Long before there were ever any homes here on Pearl Island, it was a playground for the animals and people of the sea. Ships would come and anchor before they continued onto the next phase of their trip, and they always spoke of mermaids they had seen at sea. The sea lions and dolphins were in abundance, and everything was perfect until one man appeared. There was nothing wrong with the man; he had done nothing except to have two mermaids fall in love with him. One loved him with all her heart; the other loved him more as a means of controlling the human's soul."

Morgan rocked in the rocking chair a little harder until the cat dug her claws into her leg to remind her she had a passenger. Giving the cat an apologetic pat, Morgan continued.

"He returned the love of one mermaid, Keyna, but his love was causing a rift in the kingdom, a rift that could turn and destroy the island. One night the man came to the shore to tell Keyna that she was the one he chose. But both mermaids were there. When he proclaimed his love for Keyna, the second mermaid grew furious and threatened to destroy both him and all who inhabited the island unless Keyna agreed to leave the island and never return. She agreed and left her lover, but now the second mermaid wanted nothing to do with the man. He had refused her, and she could never forgive him for that. He was now her mortal enemy. Keyna knew she could never let him die because she loved him. The mermaids made a bargain, and Keyna gave up her life around the island to allow the human to live. As she said her goodbyes to the human, great tears fell from her eyes, forming magnificent pearls. Before she left, she picked one pearl from the ocean and gave it to him, telling him it would always protect him and his ancestors. Then she dove into the sea, never to be seen again. Angry that she had lost, the second mermaid threatened the man, promising he would always be tied to the island; he and his ancestors. And if they ever left, she would come back and destroy the island and all its inhabitants."

Misty reached a paw up to pat Morgan's cheek as if in comfort. Morgan wiped the tears and looked back towards the ocean. Standing in front of her was Dylan and the shimmering figure of her aunt.

"You've remembered, haven't you?" Dylan asked, walking up the stairs to stand at her side.

Meredith smiled sadly but said nothing.

Morgan looked directly at her aunt, nodding. "The man, the one the mermaids fought over...he was the Seaver, wasn't he? That's why I've always been called to the shore, always called to return home. Isn't it, Aunt Meredith?"

But before Morgan could get an answer from either of them, she felt a tingling in her finger, and she looked down and watched in astonishment as the shell on her ring opened to reveal the pearl, its colors even more intense than the first time she had seen it. Morgan felt the intensity of the colors vibrate throughout her body as if she was absorbing their power. It was over in an instant, and when she looked back down at the ring, the shell had closed.

Meredith reached out a hand as if she was going to push the hair back from Morgan's face, but she hesitated and looked over at Dylan.

"It's starting, Morgan. The ring is giving you your powers; it has put its mark on you," Meredith whispered.

"What do you mean, putting its mark on me?" Morgan looked over at Dylan for an answer.

"Look at your reflection in the window, Morgan," was all Dylan said, pointing to the window.

Morgan jumped to her feet, dropping the kitten in the chair as she did and turned to the window. There was just enough reflection for her to see that the blue streaks in her hair had changed from a deep blue into a more aqua color, shimmering just as the pearl had. Morgan turned back to demand an answer, but her aunt was gone.

Dylan gave a shrug of his shoulders. "I can't give you all the answers, Morgan. But I can tell you this; you need to be careful. You are the last Seaver. Whoever killed your aunt made sure of that. More than the Seaver legacy is at stake. I fear that it would be chaos on the island if there was no one from your family line to protect the island."

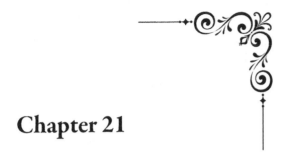

Chapter 21

M organ had tried to press Dylan for more information, but he
wasn't forthcoming. He didn't stay much longer after Meredith
disappeared, and it left Morgan to ponder her memories.

It was Gabe who showed up at lunch instead of Dylan and,
although Morgan was happy to see the younger man, she missed her
lunchtime with Dylan. She'd gotten in the habit of spending a quiet
meal with the older man, talking about her aunt, or about life in
general. He was her connection to Meredith, knowing her both as a
friend and Morgan was guessing, as a lover.

The lunch with Gabe was full of laughter and jokes, and she had
needed that. As he was leaving, the post-woman showed up with a large
package, and Gabe had helped the woman carry it up the porch stairs.
Then he had taken it and put it in Morgan's workroom for her and
watched as she happily unwrapped it.

Inside was a stack of old books. On top was a note from a repeat
customer pleading Morgan to put all her attention on the books; they
were his wife's birthday gift. It didn't take much for Gabe to see Morgan
was eager to start on the project, and he'd left shortly after. It thrilled
Morgan to see the box, to be honest, as she was feeling like she was
losing connection with her old life.

The island and her new life were so different from what she was
used to. She carefully unwrapped the books, placing them on the
worktable she had set up. Then she shooed Misty out of the room
before the kitten could get into any trouble and started exploring the

work that needed her attention. She lost hours working, and before she knew it, she had to turn on the lights in the room to accommodate for the darkening sky outside.

Morgan was occupied with the books for the next three days. Gabriel and Dylan both popped in to check on her but gave her the space she needed.

By the third day, Morgan had finished her task, pleased with the results. She boxed the books up carefully and arranged for someone from the post office to come and pick them up for her. Walking the box out to the porch where they would be picked up, she looked out towards the ocean and saw Dylan walking, his head held low.

She realized with a start that she had not really seen much of him other than the occasional meal. She'd been so wrapped up in her work that she hadn't given it a second thought, but now she remembered seeing him walk the beach from the windows. She wondered if he felt closer to her aunt as he walked the shore. Morgan knew she did; she always felt more complete when she was near the water.

Meredith had made an appearance once or twice over the last few days, as if she was checking in to make sure her niece was okay, but she didn't stay. She'd seemed satisfied to see Morgan busy.

But now the job was completed, and Morgan knew she had to search the library for answers to the questions she had about her family history.

Dusk had settled, and the twilight was deepening. Morgan looked out the window and tried to ignore the irresistible urge to walk on the shore. They had warned her to be careful, but she saw Dylan walk the coast without a problem, and there had been no other threats from Stanley. Her alibi was solid, and no matter how hard he tried, the officer could not arrest her or even pin the blame on her. Morgan had caught his furious look the few times she'd gone into town, but she ignored him, hoping it would all blow over.

Not bothering to lock the door behind her, Morgan started down the pathway to the shore. She had no need for a flashlight; the moon was high in the sky, casting a brilliant glow on the sand beneath it. The wind had picked up considerably, and the waves were crashing against the shore. Jenny had pointed out a few spots right offshore to be careful of. It was deceptive looking because there was a huge drop off at one point, unnoticeable until you took that step and plunged into the water below. Morgan had listened to the radio earlier and knew there was also a threat of riptides. It was an evening to stay out of the water and on dry land. She walked in the opposite direction where she usually went, not thinking about it, just putting one foot in front of the other.

"Morgan."

Morgan's head jerked up at the sound of the threatening female voice, and she looked around to see where it had come from.

Sirena was standing right on the edge of the shore, her feet getting wet by the rough waves crashing against the sand.

"What do you want, Sirena? I have nothing to say to you. Why are you here? Is there something else you'd like to accuse me of?"

Morgan was surprised at the combative tone in her own voice. It was unusual for her, but Sirena had pushed her to her limit. She knew darn well the young woman had been spreading lies about her on the island, and she was using Stanley to help her. Jenny had done her best to come between the two women, but Morgan was still furious about the vandalism to her bike. She even asked Jenny if there was a possibility that Sirena had been the one to kill her aunt. She remembered the strange look Jenny had thrown her way, but she hadn't answered her. It wasn't until later that Morgan found out Jenny was pursuing that idea.

"You don't belong here, Morgan. The island doesn't need the Seavers anymore. Why don't you leave before it's too late?"

"Is that a threat, Sirena? If you're so against the Seaver family, then tell me this: did you have something to do with my aunt's death?"

The wild gust of wind blew the other woman's long red curls in all directions like a tangled mass of seaweed. She made a grim picture as the moonlight seem to capture her in this spotlight.

Sirena looked at Morgan for a moment before bursting out laughing, delighted with what Morgan said. "So, you think I had something to do with your aunt's death? We warned her to leave the island. But she didn't listen; she didn't understand your family's time is over."

Morgan's fist clenched, and she took an aggressive step forward, ready to challenge the other woman. "And who are you to tell me this? What do you know about my family or my family's history? You didn't answer my question, Sirena. What do you know about my aunt's death?"

The other girl just laughed hysterically as if she knew some destructive secrets that she wasn't willing to share. She made a motion with her hand as if daring Morgan to come forward and confront her face-to-face. Morgan took a few more steps in her direction, her anger taking over her better judgment. Behind Sirena, the waves were crashing wildly, each one getting taller as it hit the shoreline. And around Morgan, a mist was developing, a thick mist, thicker than she'd seen before on the island.

It seemed like two forces of nature were about to meet head-on, instigated by the two women facing each other. There were only five or six feet between the two of them.

Sirena raised her arms above her head as if she was summoning something from the deep sea. There was a deep roaring in Morgan's ears, and she braced herself, expecting an attack.

"No, stop!"

Sirena's arms dropped to her side in surprise, and both women turned in the direction of the voice crying out from the dunes. They watched, astonished, as the figure of an older man came running full force. Sirena quickly raised her hands as if she would attack again, but she wasn't fast enough. The man was almost on top of her. To save herself from being knocked over, she took a step to the side. But Dylan was running too hard and too fast to correct his momentum. Before he could stop himself, he landed in the water.

Morgan watched, horrified, as he disappeared from sight. He'd fallen into one of the drop-offs that she'd been warned against. Behind her, there were shouts from others rushing towards them, and Sirena turned and ran in the opposite direction to save herself. Morgan knew she wasn't a strong enough swimmer to jump into the deep water and search for Dylan. She scanned the horizon, hoping the moonlight would illuminate him as he surfaced.

Clouds shifted, and now she could see his head surface. She turned to Gabe and Jenny as they reached her side, pointing in Dylan's direction.

"Dylan went into the drop-off. I'm not a good enough swimmer to save him. Please hurry."

Gabe was stripping off his clothes as she spoke, but before he could jump in after his uncle, Jenny grabbed his arm, holding him back. She pointed at the water, and they followed her pointing finger. At first, Morgan didn't know what she was seeing. Then she realized that Dylan was caught in an overpowering riptide. If any of them jumped in, it would also capture them, and it would drag them under. He surfaced one more time looking in their direction, and then he disappeared. Morgan turned her head away from the water, not wanting to see anymore, knowing that it was too late. As she turned, she saw a glimmering figure on the widow's walk and knew her aunt was also watching.

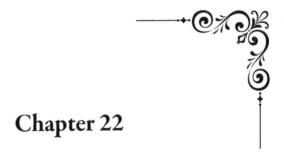

Chapter 22

Jenny was quick to act, even though Morgan was sure it was a lost cause. She radioed for help, and within half an hour, the Coast Guard was offshore searching. The waves had died down enough to allow for safe rescue, and the mist had all but disappeared, but it was to no avail. Dylan was lost to them.

Gabe sat on the shore watching the activities of the rescuers, his shoulders hunched in defeat. Morgan dropped to the sand to sit next to him, putting her arms around him in comfort, as one might a small child.

Others from the island came to the shore to see what was going on, standing in small circles watching and talking, knowing there would be no rescue.

It was Winnie and Kathy who convinced Morgan and Gabe to go back up to the house. The search was entering its second hour, and Winnie had enough years of experience with tragedies along the shore to know they would find nothing tonight.

Morgan and Gabe couldn't bring themselves to go inside the house. Instead, they sat on a couch on the porch where they could still watch the activity going down on the beach. Kathy urged them inside, but Winnie gave her a sharp shake of her head. Motioning for her granddaughter to follow her, Winnie led the way inside to the kitchen and went about making a pot of coffee and some sandwiches. Even if Morgan and Gabe weren't hungry, the actions of holding a cup and eating would take their mind off Dylan, if only for a few moments.

While the two women were inside, Gabe finally looked at Morgan, squeezing her hand.

"What happened down there? I only saw part of it. Was it Sirena I saw running away?" Gabe asked.

"Yes, it was Sirena. She was looking for a confrontation with me. But it was like no other confrontation I'd ever seen. She was possessed, with no regard for her own safety, let alone anyone else's. If I'd taken one more step towards her then she would have taken one back in defense. It would've been her that would have gone over the edge, not— "

"But she was threatening you?"

"Yes, and I'll be honest, it scared me. I didn't know what Sirena was going to do; attack me or what. And then Dylan just came out of nowhere. He saved me, Gabe."

Gabe was silent for a moment and then slowly nodded, giving her a weak smile. "Yes, he did. And it's the way it was supposed to be. By saving you, Uncle Dylan redeemed himself for letting Meredith die."

Morgan looked sharply at the man sitting next to her, taken back by his words. "Dylan did not let Meredith die. Someone with evil in their heart killed my aunt, and they did it on purpose. There was nothing anybody could have done to stop it. I don't know why you and Dylan both thought he could've prevented it."

Gabe reached out and caught her hands in his, offering her the comfort that she had just provided him. "There are still things you don't understand."

"I understand a lot of things and the biggest one is that there is evil on this island, an evil that I don't remember being here as a child." Morgan shook away his hands and stood up. "This evil on the island isn't from some long-ago legend. No, I'm afraid it's from the hands of somebody who had it in for my aunt, and I have every intention of figuring out who it is. Sirena has something to do with this."

Kathy and Winnie came out as Morgan was finishing her statement, but they said nothing, just handed out the coffee. Winnie stood there and looked at the two of them for a moment. She seemed to size them up before she added her own advice.

"If the two of you want to figure out who killed Meredith, then you need to work together. Gabe, you know as well as I do your family has always looked out for the Seavers, and you're strongest when you work as one. Morgan's right; it was human hands that killed Meredith. And whoever it was is still loose on the island."

"Granny, come on, you know Jenny doesn't want us to get involved," Kathy cautioned.

"Nonsense. Jenny may be in charge of this case, but you know as well as I do that it's not some outsider who has come as a tourist to do this harm. It's one of our own who's turned bad, and we need to find him or her before more destruction happens."

Winnie sat down on the chair with her arms folded across her chest in defiance, daring her granddaughter to contradict her.

Gabe looked at the three women sharing the porch with him and sighed. They were right. But he couldn't think of that now, not until after they had made every attempt to recover his uncle. He wouldn't allow himself to be deterred.

Gabe never left the porch that night, watching the goings-on down on the beach, answering questions as people came up to offer comfort to him. And Morgan sat by his side the entire time. It wasn't until the sun rose that Jenny came to them, and they knew the search had been called off.

Dylan was still missing.

Chapter 23

It had been almost a week since that night on the beach, and slowly things were getting back to normal for Morgan and the island community. Gabe was dealing with his grief in his own silent way, and Morgan found the best thing she could do was to be there to offer him support. When he was ready to talk, she would listen.

Meredith had come to Morgan during the week, letting her know that Dylan was in a place safe from harm and was content. Tentatively, Morgan passed that message on to Gabe, and it seemed to be what Gabe had needed to hear. It was as though he knew that the destiny of his uncle's was just as his would be, and he accepted it.

While Gabe was dealing with the loss of his uncle, Morgan thought of the events since her arrival at Pearl Island. She was convinced that Stanley was impeding Jenny's investigation into Meredith's murder.

Gabe and Morgan were sitting on the outcropping of rocks that had become they're favorite place. They'd been spending a lot of time together, but Morgan hadn't brought up the events that had changed both of their lives so drastically the night Dylan died.

Instead, it was Gabe who did as they sat there. "That night on the beach, you told me what happened between you and Sirena. Did anything else happen? Was there anybody else around?"

Morgan shook her head, but her movement was arrested as she remembered a shadowy figure that had been watching from a distance that night.

"There was someone," she said. "I couldn't see him clearly, but I know it was a man, and he was rather large. He never came forward to help."

"What happened to him?"

"I don't know. Things happened so fast; I never saw him after that first glance. I don't know if he left before Dylan arrived or after. He just disappeared."

"Do you think he left with Sirena?"

She thought about his question for a moment and then gave a shrug. "It's possible. It's probable. Sirena just disappeared that night too; she must've had help. But who?"

The two were silent for a moment, thinking about Morgan's answers. Then Morgan asked a question of her own. "You're close with Jenny. Has she said anything to you about the investigation?"

"Only that she's frustrated with the lack of clues and—"

"Stanley's insistence that I had something to do with it. Yeah, I know, she's told me that a couple of times," Morgan interrupted.

Gabe was silent for a moment, and when he turned to face Morgan, she could see the intensity of his eyes. "That night that Uncle Dylan disappeared, Winnie said some things, things that I dismissed at the time. But she was right. We need to figure out who killed your aunt and we need to work together to do it."

Morgan could see he'd given it some thought and was ready to move on. Having something constructive to do was the perfect antidote to the grief he still felt. The grief Morgan also felt. Yes, being busy would help the two of them, and if in the process they could find who killed Meredith, that was even better.

"Okay, so where do we start?" Morgan asked.

"With the only one who will give us a straight answer." Gabe smiled back at her.

"If you mean Meredith, I tried. She never saw who attacked her. And I guess it took a while for her to become whatever it is that she is now."

"You can say ghost, Morgan." Gabe laughed out loud. "I hadn't even thought about Meredith. I was talking about Jenny. If there are any facts, she has them. And I think she's frustrated enough with her partner that she might accept some extra help."

Morgan rolled her eyes at his answer. She still hadn't been able to admit the Meredith who came to her now was a ghost. But there really wasn't any other explanation, was there?

ONCE MORGAN AND GABE decided the next step was to question Jenny, they lost no time and headed towards town, leaving a sleepy Misty on the couch. The kitten barely opened one eye as they went, merely giving a twitch of her tail to acknowledge them. They cut through the gardens to Main Street and the post office, which also held an office for the police.

As they walked, several islanders' expressed condolences to both as they greeted them. Many went out of their way to tell Morgan they were happy she was staying on the island. She was beginning to feel a sense of home, and the greetings from the Islanders made her feel even more welcomed. It was a beautiful day, and they walked at a slow pace, enjoying each other's company, not talking much. Occasionally their hands would touch as they walked, and Morgan would look at Gabe, wondering what it would be like if he reached out and grabbed her hand. But she pushed that thought out of her head; other things needed to be concentrated on. Things that were important, and daydreaming would not get them accomplished.

When they opened the door to the post office, they were greeted by Jill Thomas, the postmistress, and the woman who'd picked up a box of books that Morgan had shipped out earlier in the week. Morgan thanked the woman for her service, letting her know that the customer had gotten the box in perfect condition.

"I really appreciate your help in getting that box out. That is an important part of my business, and it's nice to know that you cared enough to make sure the shipment was handled properly."

"Not a problem, I was happy to help. It was nice to be up to the Seaver beach house. I hadn't been there in a long time. Any time you need something like that, just call me. I can be there within a couple of hours," Jill assured Morgan. Morgan suspected that the woman looked forward to getting out of the small office occasionally.

They chatted for a few moments, and then Gabe asked if Jenny was around. But before she answered him, the door opened, and Stanley entered the room.

"What do you want?"

"They're here looking for Jenny. Have you seen her?" Jill jumped in, answering for them.

Stanley glared at the two of them, and Morgan was grateful for Gabe's company, and that she hadn't tried to come by herself.

"The only reason you should be standing here in this office, Miss Seaver, is because you've come to admit your guilt. Ready to admit that you killed your aunt and turn yourself in?" Stanley sneered.

The woman behind the counter gasped, and there was a shocked silence from the others. The venom in his voice was overwhelming, but Morgan refused to be intimidated.

She stood taller and glared right back at the man. "Sorry to disappoint you. I'm not here to admit anything, because I didn't do anything. When are you going to get over this? I've proven my innocence!"

"Yeah, well, I'm not convinced. Somehow you've manipulated the facts in your favor."

Stanley glared back at her, trying to intimidate her. But when that didn't work, he walked into his small office, slamming the door behind him. There was a stunned silence as the three of them stared at the closed door. Then Jill picked up a piece of paper and tried to laugh it off.

"You wouldn't know it by his actions, but that guy there is pretty nice. Maybe you've just caught him on a bad day."

"Does he ever have a good day?" Morgan mumbled.

The three of them laughed, breaking the tension, and Jill picked up the phone on her desk and shot off a quick text message to Jenny. A few moments later, she looked back at the other two with a smile.

"Jenny's down at the docks. She said for you to meet her down there."

"Thanks, Jill. I hope Stanley calms down and isn't a grouch all day to you," said Gabe.

"Oh, don't worry about him. Things will work out. You two have a good day." The woman assured Gabe she wasn't worried and waved them out the door.

Chapter 24

Morgan and Gabe stood outside the closed door looking at each other, debating what to do. The docks were at the other end of the island where the ferry came in, and although it wasn't a great distance, the four and a half miles would take too long to walk, and they would chance missing Jenny.

"Come on, I have an idea."

Making a quick decision, Gabe grabbed Morgan's hand and dragged her along behind him. A few moments later, they walked up the sidewalk to his small townhouse. They paused only long enough for him to take her around the side of the house and show her his newest toy, a beautiful twin-engine boat., hooked up to the trailer waiting to take its first dip in the ocean. Morgan made all the appropriate ooh and aahs before Gabe grabbed the keys to his car, and they jumped in, heading down to the docks.

They arrived at the end of the island where the ferry docked at the commercial end of the island. Tourists rarely came down this far. It was for residents and suppliers bringing in items needed by those living and working on the island or for residents coming and going to the mainland to their jobs. The tourists used the other end, coming over the quaint one-lane bridge onto the island.

Gabe parked the car in the municipal parking area, and as Morgan got out with him, she put her hands up to shading her eyes from the glare of the sun and started looking for Jenny.

"There she is, down on the dock," Morgan dropped her hand from her forehead and pointed to where Jenny was. The other woman saw the two of them and waved, motioning for them to join her at the boat.

"What are you two up to?" Jenny asked as they walked down the dock to the boat.

"I almost hate to ask, there's been so much going on, but Jenny, are there any new leads on my aunt's death? Anything that might lead to her killer?" Morgan didn't waste time with pleasantries; instead, she jumped right in asking what was on her mind.

Jenny didn't answer right away. Instead, she looked around as if to see if there was somebody that might eavesdrop on their conversation.

"Why don't you two jump in and we'll take a spin on the water? We can talk freely out there," Jenny suggested.

Gabe looked like he was ready to jump right in the boat, but Morgan took a step back, and the two of them looked at her questioningly.

"You know, I kinda like to keep my feet on dry ground," she said apologetically.

The other two looked at her, astonished.

Then Jenny gave a short laugh. "The Seaver who is afraid of the water? Doesn't that go against everything ingrained in your blood? What about all the legends?"

Morgan didn't answer at first, embarrassment holding her tongue. Then she lifted her chin defiantly. "I'm not afraid of the water. I love the water. But I prefer to be on the shore looking at the ocean. I've never been able to enjoy being on a boat. Don't know why, but there it is."

Gabe jumped to her defense and suggested they sit at one of the benches lining the edges of the dock. She caught his longing look at the boat and knew he wanted to go out with Jenny on the water.

"Go, Gabe, I can sit here and wait."

But Gabe shook his head and held his hand out for Jenny to help her out of the boat. Then he led the way to sit next to each of the women on the bench. They were silent for a moment, and then Morgan repeated her question.

"You would think I would have some leads." The frustration was easy to hear in Jenny's voice. "But it seems like every time I get somewhere, the avenue I was going is closed, or information is missing, or someone doesn't want to talk. It's almost as if there is a person behind the scenes who is trying to stop me from finding Meredith's killer. But don't worry, I will."

Morgan was silent. She had her own thoughts on what was going on, but she didn't want to offend Jenny by making a wrong suggestion.

Finally, she cleared her throat and turned so she could clearly see Jenny's face as she spoke to her. "What if I start looking into her death?" Morgan held her hands up stop Jenny from interrupting her, and then continued. "If somebody is trying to stop you, they're not going to think anything of me asking questions. After all, Meredith was my aunt; I should be asking questions. And maybe people will be more forthcoming talking to a relative rather than the police. I promise I'll be careful."

Jenny looked back and forth between the two of them and seemed to come to a decision. "Gabe, you have to promise to be with her at all times when she's putting her nose in things she shouldn't be. And according to the legend, isn't that what you're supposed to do, anyway?"

Gabe nodded, but before he could say anything, Morgan butted in. "Does everything on this island revolve around legends? Doesn't anything happen normally? I don't remember ever hearing about a Seaver needing a guardian. I can take care of myself, you know. I've been doing it for years."

Morgan jumped to her feet in anger as she spoke, glaring at the two sitting in front of her. She'd just about had enough of all this talk of legends, even though in her heart she knew there was something to it.

Gabe waited until she got it out of her system, and then he reached up and grabbed her hand, pulling her back down to sit next to him.

"Of course, you can take care of yourself," he said. "But Jenny's right. Regardless of legends, what you believe or don't believe, there's a killer on this island. One that hasn't been caught. You need to be careful, and you need to have somebody at your back. If it was me, I would expect somebody to have my back."

"Look, you two talk this out," Jenny said. "Gabe, if you want to go out on the water with me, I'm leaving in five minutes. We won't be long, Morgan, if you want to wait. There's a nice beach area on the other side of the dock that you might want to walk." Jenny got to her feet, ready to go back to her boat. But she looked at Gabe and offered a suggestion. "You might want to tell her the rest of the legend, Gabe."

The two of them were silent as he watched Jenny walk back to her boat and hop in.

Then Morgan turned to the man next to her and apologized for being so short with him. "Jenny's right, and so were you. If we work together, it will be safer." She hesitated for a moment, "With everything I've heard about the legend, I've never heard about the Seavers having a guardian."

Gabe gave her a quick hug, pleased that she was agreeable. Then, seeing her questioning look, told her his part of the legend.

"When the first Seaver was being fought over by two mermaids, he had a best friend," he said. "Another man his own age, and they shared everything. This man knew of his love of the mermaid, but he also knew of the danger, something the first Seaver refused to see. When the mermaid, Keyna, gave up her love, she entrusted the best friend to always look after her lover. It was his family's destiny. It was my family's destiny."

Morgan gasped and looked up at him, but he continued before she could ask him questions.

"There has always been a member of my family looking out for the Seavers. Uncle Dylan and Meredith were inseparable for more than one reason. It was their destiny."

"So, you're saying that we're basing our friendship on a legend?" Morgan gave a shake of her head and looked at him with a spark of anger. "That's the only reason we have this special bond that I've been feeling?" Angrily she wiped away the small tear forming in the corner of her eye.

"Morgan, you know as well as I do, legend or not, that we were meant to know each other. And the friendship that we have goes beyond legends and destiny. I would have been drawn to you regardless of where we met or how we connected."

The two of them sat and stared at each other. Then Morgan seemed to accept his words, and she reached out and gave him a quick hug.

"You're right. And who are we to question the friendship that Uncle Dylan and Meredith had? It was deeper than anything I've ever seen."

Gabe cleared his throat and looked over to the boat where Jenny was standing, her arms crossed over her chest, getting inpatient.

Morgan followed his glance and laughed. "Go for your boat ride. Maybe you can pump Jenny for more information, find out what clues she's been stumbling over."

"Are you sure? I can go with her any time."

"No, now's the time before Jenny changes her mind and won't let us help. I'll take a walk along the shore. I'll wait for you there."

Chapter 25

Morgan watched Gabe cast off the lines and jump in the boat. She returned Jenny's wave as the two of them headed out to sea. She knew without being told that Jenny would take the boat out to the area where the search for Dylan had ended. Kathy had been the one to tell Morgan that Jenny, Gabe, and a few others went out searching every morning. Gabe had been quiet about the disappearance of his uncle, and Morgan could tell he was silently grieving. She had met his cousins and an aunt and uncle on the day they held a prayer vigil for Dylan, and she was glad to know Gabe had family around to offer him comfort.

Morgan watched a couple of boats return from the sea and moor at the dock. For a small island community, there always seemed to be an activity to capture your interest. Morgan enjoyed the contrast from one end of the island to the other. Like the sea, nothing ever seemed to settle or go stagnant. She found she was looking forward to becoming a part of island life.

Getting up from the bench, Morgan walked to the railing and looked down at the beach below. She had spent little time at this end of the island, and it surprised her to see a group of ATVs (All-Terrain Vehicles) racing up and down the sand. They were being driven by teenagers, who were being respectful of the people who were bathing along the shore. The ATVs kept close to the loose sand, letting the area immediately at the water's edge alone for the sunbathers. She could hear the laughter and shouts to each other over the sound of the engines, and she couldn't help but smile at the enjoyment the kids were getting out of their afternoon activities. Morgan watched for a few moments then took the stairs down to the beach to wander while she waited for Jenny and Gabe to return.

She was pleased when she was greeted by two beachgoers, and she recognized them from her aunt's memorial service. She returned their waves but didn't stop to talk. Morgan had too many things to think about.

The number one thing on her mind was the fact that Jenny was getting nowhere with the case. She was sure someone was trying to stop the discovery of the killer. And whoever it was, they were still trying to put the blame on Morgan. At least according to Stanley, they were.

"Stanley..." Morgan came to a standstill as she thought about the other officer, wondering what he had against her. She'd never seen him before coming to the island, and she'd never heard her aunt complain about any problems with anyone either. Morgan thought about the man's accusations, even in the face of evidence that had cleared her. It was like he was on a one-track destination and wasn't allowing for anything to deter him from his final point. And Morgan was afraid she was that last point. It would be up to her and Gabe to find substantial evidence to prove he was wrong and to find her aunt's killer.

Morgan had been so involved in her own thoughts that she didn't realize how far she'd wandered down the beach. It was easy to get lost in her thoughts. The call of the seagulls and the muted voices of the others on the beach made for the perfect environment for deep reflection. With a start, she realized there weren't very many people around her, and she turned to head back towards the pier. She noticed that most of the ATVs were parked, and the group of teenagers was gathered by the shore, listening to music and talking. She walked at a brisk pace, and before long, she was close to the kids. She passed them with a wave and picked up her pace, realizing that Gabe and Jenny should be back. She kept her eye on the sand as she walked, noticing the small footprints in the wet sand. They belonged to the small sea terns that ran back and forth on the water's edge as if they were playing a game of chicken with the waves. Morgan was getting closer to the pier when she noticed something in the sand. Looking closer, she was pleased to find a perfectly shaped starfish. She bent down and grabbed it but straightened quickly when she heard voices yelling.

"Morgan! Look out."

Morgan looked up towards the pier, recognizing Gabe's voice. But she wasn't fast enough, and she felt the force of something pushing her off her feet and the roar of a machine close by. Gabe's shout had alerted the others, and they came running to her rescue. Morgan watched in disbelief as an ATV kept driving past her, racing at full speed under the pier and disappearing.

Chapter 26

Morgan felt strong arms help her to her feet. She looked at the young men who had been driving the other ATVs, now staring at her with concern.

"Are you okay, Miss?" The oldest of the teenagers helped her to her feet. His question brought her attention back to the here and now. She started to answer him and then felt the pain in her side where she'd been pushed hard.

"Thank you. Honestly, I'm fine. I'll be bruised, but it's not a big deal. Do you all know who was riding that vehicle?"

By now, Gabe and Jenny had joined them. Jenny pulled out her badge and started asking questions in an official tone. The teenagers were polite, but unfortunately, they had no answers. They didn't know the driver of the other ATV, and they didn't know when he had shown up. He wasn't part of their group.

As Jenny questioned the teens, Gabe made Morgan sit down on the sand. Gently he pulled her shirt up on the side where he could see where her assailant made contact. Already a large round bruise was forming.

Morgan looked down at her side and frowned. "What in the world did he push me with?"

Gabe was silent for a moment as he looked at the bruise, but when he looked up, Morgan saw the anger on his face.

"Are you sure the rider was male?" Gabe asked. "From the size and shape of that bruise, I would almost guess whoever pushed you had a boxing glove on."

"I assumed it was a guy, but now that you asked, I can't be positive. But he was pretty accurate on that ATV. But he was leaning way off to the side, as if he had to stretch to push me over." Morgan looked at Gabe with her eyebrows raised in question. "What makes you think it was a boxing glove?"

Gabe gave her a wry grin. "I've had that bruise on me half a dozen times and recognize it. We've got a good kickboxing team here on the island. And the members are both male and female; that's why I asked if you were sure it was a male."

Before Morgan could answer, Jenny came over to join them. She'd finished with her questions and taking down information from those who had helped Morgan. Now she was looking at the bruise on Morgan's side.

"Gabe, you better get her over to Dr. Wright. Make sure there's no damage to her kidneys. That bruise is right in that area." Morgan tried to protest that she was fine, but when she stood up, the pain made her double over. Jenny just shook her head, as if to say I told you so. Gabe didn't give her a chance to protest any further and wrapped his arms around her, being careful of the injured area. Ten minutes later, he was pulling up in front of a private residence.

Before Gabe could get out and open the door for Morgan, a man, so tall and skinny he looked like he could be walking on stilts, was at the car helping her out. Standing in the doorway of the house was a woman as plump as the man was skinny. Dr. Wright and his wife were home and ready to help. Jenny must have called ahead to let them know they were coming. In a matter of minutes, Morgan was in his home office, and he was tutting over her injury. While he saw to Morgan, Mrs. Wright was putting Gabe at ease and making tea for all of them.

"She will be a bit sore but otherwise no major problems." The doctor and Morgan had come out from his office to the kitchen, and Dr. Wright clapped his hand on Gabe's shoulder in reassurance.

"Good, Mother, I see you made some tea. That's the perfect medicine right now; strong sweet tea." Holding the chair out for Morgan, the doctor made her sit down while Mrs. Wright fussed, pouring a hot cup of sweet tea and placing it in front of her.

Mrs. Wright was a chatterbox and, even though her husband tried to tone her down, she was livid that somebody had tried to hurt Morgan.

"I've never seen people on this island act so foolishly before. Running over people with machinery, accusing you of murdering your own aunt. Believe me, Morgan, this is not how the citizens of Pearl Island act. There's a bad penny in the lot, and the sooner they're found, the better. I, for one, will be happy to go back to my normal life and not have to look over my shoulder, wondering if there's a killer out there."

"Now, Mother. You need not carry on like that. Morgan had a shakeup; she doesn't need to hear your take on our island life," admonished her husband.

Morgan smiled at the two. She couldn't help it; they were so cute together. As they talked, she noticed that they finished each other's sentences and anticipated each other's needs. She watched as Dr. Wright spooned in the sugar for his wife's tea, while she reached over and dabbed at the tiny mess he had made in front of him. Their interactions with each other were putting Morgan at ease.

Her side hurt like the dickens, but the doctor had given her something for the pain, and it was starting to work. Dr. Wright refused to let her leave his house until he was sure she was okay. They spent the next half hour talking about the day's events. They had moved from the kitchen table to the living room. Mrs. Wright made sure Morgan was sitting in a comfortable chair with her feet up.

Between the comfort of the chair and the medicine, Morgan was drifting off. But then she saw something shimmering in the room's corner, and she looked over, thinking it was a reflection in the mirror. But instead of her reflection, she saw the shimmering form of her Aunt Meredith. There was concern in her aunt's eyes. Through the grogginess, Morgan heard her aunt's voice warn her she needed to get back to the beach house.

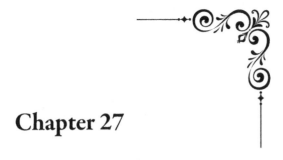

Chapter 27

Morgan closed her eyes just for a moment, but it was long enough for Meredith to disappear. She wondered if her aunt had ever really been there because there was no reaction from the others in the room. But then Morgan remembered the warning, and she had a feeling Meredith meant the message for only her.

Her aunt wanted her to be at the beach house. Something was happening, and she forced herself to shake off the grogginess. Sitting straight up in the chair, she moved her feet off the footstool, catching the attention of the others. Mrs. Wright fussed, but the doctor intervened.

"Now, Mother, we've done our job here. It looks like Morgan is ready to head home."

The doctor knew how to read his patients, and he understood trying to persuade Morgan to stay any longer would be worthless. He motioned for Gabe to help Morgan out of the chair.

"You will be sore for a couple of days, but that should ease off," Dr. Wright said. "I don't see any reason for you to have to limit your activity or pamper yourself any more than you need to. As a matter of fact, the best thing you can do is continue to move around, so you don't get stiff. But I don't want you to overdo it." The doctor gave her a firm but friendly smile and then turned to Gabe with his instructions.

"Our friend here might be more comfortable on the first floor, rather than trying to walk upstairs for the rest of the day while that medicine works its way through her. You've been through this before,

Gabe, and you know how sore she will be, but it won't last long. Now the two of you skedaddle. Morgan, if you need anything, Gabe has my number."

Morgan thanked the Wrights for their hospitality and help, and then let Gabe help her to the car. The doctor and his wife waved from the doorway and then went back into the house. But Gabe didn't start the car. Instead, he turned to Morgan.

"What's going on? You got anxious to leave all of a sudden in there."

"You can think I'm nuts, but I saw Meredith," she told him. "She wasn't fully there, but I saw her, and even though she didn't say it, I heard her warn me to get home. I don't know what's going on at the house, but she wants me there."

Gabe nodded, not questioning her instincts. He put the car in gear and started towards the beach house. Driving the main road through the island, it only took a few minutes before Morgan and Gabe pulled up in front of the beach house. From the street, the house looked normal. There were no broken windows and nothing was out of place, but as soon as Morgan got out of the car, she knew instinctively something was off. Moving slowly up the entry stairs with Gabe's help, she opened the front door to the house. Misty was sitting on the railing to go to the second floor, guarding the front door, and she meowed at the two of them as if scolding them for not being home.

Gabe began firing off instructions. "You stay here. I'll run upstairs, look around quickly and see if anything's wrong. We'll look downstairs together; just stay right where you're at. And keep that cat from tripping me." He started up the stairs only to have to do a double step as Misty jumped off the railing. Morgan didn't bother to argue over his bossiness.

It didn't take long for Gabe to come back down the stairs. With a shrug of his shoulders, he informed her that everything was fine upstairs.

"Whatever is wrong is on the first floor, I know it. Oh no, my books!" Morgan's first thought was for the workshop she had set up and the set of books she was currently working on repairing. Moving as fast as she could, she led the way to the room. Opening the door with a hesitant hand, she let out a sigh of relief when she saw everything was just as she'd left it that morning. While she made her way to the stack of books on the worktable to reassure herself all was well, Gabe ran into the living room, family room, kitchen, and dining room but found nothing amiss there either.

"I think whatever is wrong is in Meredith's office. It's the only room left," Gabe said as he returned her side.

Without saying a word, Morgan led the way to Meredith's office. Pushing open the door, Misty was the first to rush into the room. Meredith had always left the place immaculate, but it wasn't in that state now.

The doors to the desk were hanging open, and the books were pulled off the shelves. They had broken a small window next to the lock on the door, giving whoever had entered easy access. They hadn't been careful as they searched through Meredith's office. Papers were tossed, some landing on the chair, the rest spilling onto the floor. Knickknacks lay on their side, and one of Meredith's precious mermaid figures had been smashed to smithereens.

Morgan felt her temper rise furiously at the intrusion into her home and the breakage of her aunt's belongings. She looked like she was ready to tear someone apart. Gabe silently worried about the reaction she would have if she came face to face with the intruder. He had a feeling she wouldn't hold back her anger.

"This wasn't a random break-in. They were looking for something particular, and from the scope of the damage, something small. They didn't move furniture. Look, Morgan, whoever was in here only opened drawers and picked up vessels that would hold items. No, they were looking for something specific."

"But what?" Morgan looked around the room, seeing that what Gabe had said was true. "And did they find it? Whatever it is."

Morgan started to straighten the lamp on the desk with one hand, and with the other, to right the cup Meredith had used to hold her pens and pencils. She paused before she touched either item.

"Let me help. You're not gonna be comfortable until we put this room to rights."

"No," Morgan stopped his movements with a single word, and he looked at her questioningly. "This is the second time somebody has looked through Meredith's office searching for something. And this time, they were much more aggressive. I found the ring they were looking for the first time, but this time I am making a full report. I want Jenny to take pictures of this, and I want somebody to be held accountable for the intrusion and breakage."

Morgan didn't wait for Gabe to answer. Instead, she dialed the number she was now familiar with and told Jenny what had just happened. After hearing Jenny's instructions, Morgan hung up the phone and motioned for Gabe to follow her out of the room. Closing the door behind her, she didn't notice Misty was still in the office.

"Jenny will be here shortly. In the meantime, she wanted us to stay out of the room."

"That's smart. Come on, let's see if there's any food in the kitchen."

Morgan laughed as Gabe rubbed his stomach, but when her stomach rumbled in response, she agreed.

Chapter 28

They had each grabbed something from the fridge and made their way out to the front porch to await Jenny's arrival. But Morgan wasn't expecting the second car that pulled up in front of the house just a few seconds after Jenny did.

Morgan and Gabe watched Jenny exit her car and walk to stand in front of the other vehicle, hands on her hip as if expecting a confrontation.

But when the car doors opened and the two occupants got, the confrontation didn't come from Jenny. It came from Morgan.

Stiffly getting to her feet, she made her way to the top of the porch steps glaring down at Stanley and Sirena.

"Absolutely not. I don't want her on my property. Get her out of here, Jenny." Morgan pointed her hand at Sirena, her voice angry but firm.

"She's with me." Stanley glared back at Morgan and then turned to Jenny as if daring her to contradict.

But Morgan was having nothing of it. "I don't care who she's with, this is private property. If I don't want her on it, then she needs to leave. She's not an officer of the law; she has no business being here. Why is she with you anyway?"

Morgan knew she'd gone too far with the last question, but she didn't back down when Stanley took a step in her direction.

Jenny quickly intervened. "Sirena, get back in the car. Stanley, she's right. Sirena has no reason to be here. If Morgan doesn't want her on the property, there's nothing we can do about it. Have her wait in the car while we make a report about the break-in here."

There was a standoff between the four of them. No one wanted to make the first move, and each wanted to protect their position. Finally, Jenny took a step forward and put her hand on Stanley's arm, trying to calm down the situation. But Morgan had a point: why was Sirena with her partner? Without hesitating, she questioned Stanley. He looked down at his partner before answering.

"Sirena was with me when you got their phone call. I was in the other room and heard what was going on. She was at the office trying to find out why we hadn't arrested Morgan Seaver, and she came with me when I decided to come out here and meet you to question the suspect again." Giving a violent shake to knock Jenny's hand off his arm, Stanley took a step in Morgan's direction.

Until now, Gabe had been standing at Morgan's side, not saying anything, just watching. But he stiffened and took a step closer to Morgan as Stanley moved towards the stairs. Sirena came from the other side of the car to stand next to Stanley. Jenny had had enough; this was going to get out of control too quickly.

"I can handle this. Stanley, take Sirena and leave. There is no reason to question Morgan about anything except for the break-in she just reported. Morgan is not a suspect in her aunt's murder. We have proved that. You're letting Sirena talk you in circles."

Sirena took a step towards Jenny, but Jenny merely looked at her, raising an eyebrow as if daring her to do something stupid. "I'm not joking about this, you two. Stanley, get her out of here. Sirena, you're on private property, and if Morgan wants me to arrest you for trespassing, I will."

Sirena flipped her long curls over her shoulder, and then her hand paused at her throat as she reached for something. She seemed surprised when her hand grabbed air, and she gave Stanley a panicked look. It was clear she was upset about something.

"Fine. I'll leave." She glared threateningly at Morgan before she turned to head back to the car. "But this isn't over, Morgan. Stanley will find the proof that you killed your aunt. I'm not wrong."

Sirena's sudden back down took everyone by surprise, Stanley the most. He hesitated for a moment and then he turned to Jenny.

"You should pick your friends more carefully, Jenny. You're letting this one come between you and your job." Anger made his movements stiff as he turned and joined Sirena back at the car. A few seconds later, he drove off, sand kicking out from under his wheels at the vehicles' sudden acceleration.

Jenny shook her head and sighed as she walked up to join the other two. She was ready to apologize for her partner, but before she could, Morgan spoke.

"Is he right, Jenny? Is your friendship with me putting your job in jeopardy?"

"Hardly. Besides, we have proof of your innocence. I think Stanley is putting himself in jeopardy with his association with Sirena. What was he thinking, bringing her here?" Jenny's question hung in the air, and Morgan wasn't sure if she was asking them or herself the question.

"We haven't been back in Meredith's office since we talked to you, Jenny." Gabe spoke for the first time, taking control of the situation, reminding both women of the problem at hand.

"Right." Jenny gave a quick smile and motioned for him to lead the way into the house.

Reaching the library door, Morgan started to open it. She barely got it opened when a furry blur rushed from the room, causing her to step back, startled. It took a second to realize it was Misty, and as she watched the kitten run by, she saw something hanging from her mouth.

"That cat's been thieving again. I better go check what she's got."

"Let her go." Jenny stopped her from going after Misty. "Let's take a look at what's going on in here first."

135

Morgan gave a nod of agreement, but she watched the cat disappear around the corner, wondering what she'd been up to this time.

The three of them stood in the center of Meredith's office, not saying a word, and Jenny looked around her, taking in the damage. She walked over to the broken window, noting that the glass was inside the room, proving someone had broken it from outside to get in.

"You're right. Somebody was looking for something, and the intruders were not very careful about it. Any idea if anything is missing, Morgan?"

"I haven't spent much time here, so I really don't have a good idea of what Meredith had. It still feels like her room, and I didn't want to take that away." Morgan's voice trailed off as she answered her friend. She looked around her and sighed. "But that feeling has been destroyed now, hasn't it? They took more than what they expected. They took away the essence of Meredith's room."

Without another word, Morgan left the room, leaving Gabe and Jenny to take an inventory of what the intruders had disturbed.

Chapter 29

Morgan could hear the voices as Jenny and Gabe left the office and headed to the front door. She made no effort to go downstairs to say goodbye to Jenny, sure her friend would understand.

When Morgan left the office, she had sought her natural place of solace, the library. The library offered safety for her and a feeling of contentment. And right now, she didn't feel very safe or content. Someone had invaded her home and done damage to her aunt's belongings. She was past the anger and was beginning to understand that she was in danger. For some reason, someone wanted her off Pearl Island. They were making it clear whether she was a Seaver didn't matter; she wasn't welcome.

Morgan walked around the library aimlessly when she first entered the room, and without thinking about it, picked up one journal. It was a more recent one, written from within the last 20 years. She walked over to the window seat and tucked herself into the corner of the chair as if trying to hide from sight.

There was a soft tap on the library door, and Gabe stuck his head inside, not sure if he was welcome or not. "Jenny's gone. She said she'd make a report and talk to Stanley, but she didn't hold out much hope of finding out who broke into the house. You okay?"

Morgan didn't answer Gabe at first. She simply clenched the book to her chest and looked at him. When she realized he was waiting for an answer, she nodded. It surprised her to realize that she was okay.

The few moments she'd taken for herself were what she needed to put things in perspective.

"Someone doesn't want me here on the island. But that's too bad. I'm here, this is my home now, and I'm staying. They can run me over with ATVs, and they can break into my home, but I'm fighting back."

Gabe grinned back at her, relieved that her feistiness was returning. He had been concerned when she left Meredith's office, but now realized she had just needed the time to herself.

"Okay. So how do we fight back?" He walked over to sit next to her on the bench as he asked the question. Morgan put the book down and stood up. She looked out the window before answering.

"We beat them at their own game," she said. "We find out what they're looking for and why. I don't know if it revolves around the island legends or not, but something is very real and very wrong here on the island. My aunt was murdered, her house broken into, and they have attacked me. This is not the welcome I was expecting. Nor is it the way I remember the island being when I was young. Someone has come to the island with evil in their hearts, intent on destroying my family."

"Don't be so dismissive of the legends," Gabe cautioned. "I think they will play a big factor in solving what's going on. But you're right. There is something very real happening. Where do you want to start?"

Morgan was grateful that Gabe took her seriously. And even though she had been flippant about the legends, she knew he was right. Her aunt's return to her in a ghostly form had to account for something.

"Let's start where the last incident was. Maybe as I clean up Meredith's office, I'll find something. This is the second time somebody has broken in; the first time they were searching for the ring, but Misty—" Morgan stopped mid-sentence, looking around for the kitten who was usually right at her feet. "Misty found something in the office. Maybe that's where we should start. Maybe she stole something from our intruders."

"I agree with you, that cat's trouble," Gabe answered. "But I think our priority is to secure that window in the office. I can grab my toolbox and at least put a piece of wood over the broken glass."

"You're right; security and common sense first. I can always chase after that cat later. While you get your toolbox, I'll start cleaning up the mess left behind." Morgan led the way to the door, shaking her head and mumbling under her breath as she opened it. "It's a shame they destroyed one of her figurines. Meredith would be furious if she knew."

Morgan and Gabe spent the next hour cleaning up the office and securing the courtyard door. Morgan held the wood in place while Gabe screwed it into the wooden frame. When they finished, he made a phone call to a friend, arranging for somebody to come out within the next couple of days and fix the door permanently. Morgan straightened out the paperwork and put it back on top of Meredith's desk. She wasn't sure where everything belonged; she would need to figure that out later. The figurine was swept up and thrown away, there was no fixing it, and the other knick-knacks were righted on the shelves.

As they cleaned, they searched, but they could find nothing out of the ordinary that somebody would have broken into the house to steal. "Maybe they found what they were looking for," suggested Gabe.

"I don't think so. I just have a feeling they were interrupted or gave up. I think that might be why the mermaid was smashed. There was anger in that action. And I'm guessing frustration. No, Gabe, I think whatever they're looking for is still here in the house. But I don't think it's in Meredith's office. She hid it somewhere else."

Morgan wasn't sure why she was so positive about this, but it felt right to her, and Gabe seemed to agree with her. They finish with the office, and then he glanced at the clock and frowned.

"I've got a late appointment with the family lawyer in about an hour. Do you want to come with me?"

"No, I don't need a babysitter. I'll be fine here at the house. I'll make sure to lock up after you leave. I still have plenty of work to do with my books, and maybe I'll continue searching the rest of the house." Morgan was insistent when Gabe protested but he finally gave in.

"I've no idea how long I will be. I have to go to the mainland for the appointment."

"Seriously, Gabe, I'm a big girl; I can stay in the house by myself. You go do what you need to do, and I'll see you in the morning. As a matter of fact, since you're going to the mainland, you can bring back some bagels for breakfast."

Morgan could see that Gabe was hesitant, his worry evident. She gave his shoulder a push toward the front door, and he took the hint. Making her promise once again to be careful, Gabe left.

As she watched him drive away, she exhaled a sigh of relief. She hadn't realized how closed-in she felt with all the people around her. As an introvert, she found herself worn out when she was in the company of too many people at once. This was the first time she'd felt that way around Gabe, but she attributed it to all the other events that happened that day. Now she longed for the comfort of the library, a hot cup of tea, and the missing cat.

"MISTY, KITTY-KITTY!"

Morgan had made her way into the kitchen and fixed a cup of tea and now was shaking the box of treats she had found for the cat, hoping the sound would entice the kitten to appear. Sure enough, the kitten wandered into the kitchen and meowed at her.

"And where have you been?" Morgan laughed as she picked the kitten up and wiped away some cobwebs caught on her whiskers. The kitten merely bumped her head against Morgan's chin in answer. Giving her one of the little treats she had in her hand, Morgan set the cat back down onto the floor. Misty finished her treat and Morgan called her as she headed to the library. The cat followed, swishing her tail as she walked.

Morgan was content in the library for the next couple of hours, and so was the kitten who curled up in the window seat and took a nap, as if worn out from her afternoon activities. When Morgan finished the journal she was reading, she set it down and looked over at Misty, wondering what the kitten had been up to that she'd gotten herself covered in cobwebs.

"Okay, my little friend, it's time to come clean. I saw you steal something from the library. What was it, and where have you hidden it?"

But Misty merely opened her eyes and yawned, not at all interested in Morgan's questions.

Morgan laughed at the kitten and decided that she may as well search. It was apparent the kitten would not give her any guidance. Morgan remembered where she had found Misty's first stash of stolen goods, and that was where she started.

Twenty minutes later she decided the kitten must have found a new spot because everything looked the same as when she found the ring. Sitting back on her haunches, she looked around, wondering where the kitten had gone to find a new hiding spot. Then it dawned on her there was only one room in the house that she had stayed away from. And that was her aunt's bedroom. That had to be the kitten's new hiding spot. Getting to her feet, she walked to the bedroom door and, feeling like an intruder, slowly opened it.

The room echoed her aunt's presence. Mermaids, seashells, and ocean scenes were scattered on the wall. The bed held soft blue quilts and fluffy white pillows. It was like walking into an ocean oasis. It was also just as Meredith had left it, and how Morgan remembered it from her past visits.

Morgan smiled to herself, remembering the mornings as a child when she would help her aunt make her bed, often getting buried in that quilt while her aunt tickled her. They were good memories, and she was thankful for them. Brushing a stray tear from the corner of her eye, she stepped into the room further, looking around for any visible hiding spot the kitten might have found.

"Okay, if I was that cat, where would I have hidden my newest treasure?" she mumbled to herself.

Morgan moved things around, opened the closet door, and checked out the bathroom, but nothing looked dusty enough for the cat to have picked up cobwebs. The bed was flush to the floor, with a base of built-in drawers for holding linens. It wasn't until she looked at a bookshelf that her aunt had under the window that she realized it was just enough room between the wall and the shelf for the cat to get into.

"Found it. Not so sneaky, are you, Misty?"

Morgan heard a meow behind her and turned to see the cat had followed her into the room. She was now working her way over to the same corner, and Morgan pushed her away so she could look behind the shelf. She shoved the shelf away from the wall, groaning with pain as the motion irritated her side. Sure enough, the kitten had accumulated a new stash of stolen items.

"What is with you and stealing? Where are you even finding these things?" Morgan laughed at the cat as she reached behind the shelf and began pulling out the items. It was the final item that she had to reach for that got the kitten upset. She swatted at Morgan's hand as if trying to stop her from grabbing the object.

"Stop that, you silly cat." Morgan pushed her away and grabbed the shiny chain of a necklace.

She pulled the necklace out and held it up in the light so she could see it. Goosebumps ran up and down her arm, and she gave an involuntary shudder. It was a single pearl on a chain, much like what she was wearing. But where Morgan's pearl was a brilliant blue that radiated warmth, the pearl on the necklace she held was dull and black, like a void in space. Morgan dropped the necklace on the bed, not wanting to hold it any longer than she had to. Her gaze moved from the item on the bed to the cat.

"Where did you find this? It's nothing Aunt Meredith would ever wear." But the kitten didn't meow; this time she hissed. Morgan knew the necklace did not belong to Meredith.

She thought for a few moments, and then it was like a light bulb going on. She knew where the necklace had come from. Whoever had broken into the house had lost it while they were searching her aunt's office. This had to be what she had seen the kitten run off with when she opened the office door.

Then as she stood there thinking, she remembered Sirena reaching for something around her throat. Something that wasn't there.

She knew then that Sirena had been the one in the house, the one searching for something that Meredith had hidden, the one that had lost a valued something of her own.

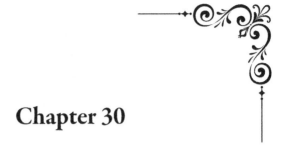

Chapter 30

Morgan stood staring down from the upper level of the widow's walk as Gabe pulled up the next morning on his bike. Instinctively he looked up and saw her, and she gave a wave before hurrying down to meet him at the front door.

When she opened the door, he was standing there grinning, holding a bag of fresh bagels in front of them. The aroma made her stomach grumble, and she grabbed his hand and dragged him into the kitchen, where she already had the coffee brewed.

Gabe laughed at her antics but joined right in, and she opened the bag of bagels, spreading cream cheese on the first one she pulled out. He reached into the cupboard and grabbed a jar of peanut butter, his choice for the bagel. Then they each poured a cup of coffee, and Morgan led the way out to the courtyard garden.

It surprised Gabe to see that she had pulled two chairs and tables from the front porch and placed them in the courtyard. She'd arranged them so that rather than being the focal point of somebody looking out from Meredith's office, they were situated so that when you walked out the second door to the courtyard, they were right there for comfort. Gabe realized the second door was where Morgan had set up her workshop, and it pleased him she was settling in so well.

"I like the quietness of the garden," Morgan explained when she saw him looking around. "One of the male peacocks even wandered in this morning. At first, his cry was annoying, but I got used to it, and he doesn't cry out that often."

As if to prove her point, one peacock flew from the gate into the courtyard. The magnificent bird looked at the two humans but didn't seem upset to find them in his area. Instead, he wandered around, opening his tail feathers as if to announce that he was accepting them.

"They're probably used to Meredith," he said. "She encouraged them to have the run of the property. The aviary she had built for them has made them feel comfortable and safe. They can actually provide some good protection for you, Morgan."

Morgan dragged her eyes away from the beautiful display from the peacock and looked at Gabe, waiting for an explanation.

"The birds will consider this their territory," he told her. "They can be very protective of it, and if they feel threatened, they will attack whoever comes in here. It's obvious they've accepted you. I've been around enough that they know my scent. Your aunt and my uncle spent a lot of time in this courtyard, and there were many times I joined them for morning coffee."

Morgan nodded and looked around the courtyard, picturing the three of them sitting around drinking coffee. She smiled at the picture in her mind.

"I was thinking of adding a water feature to the courtyard. I'm sure the birds would love to have fresh water, and I love the sound of a waterfall. As much as I love the ocean, there's something different about the trickling of water versus the waves. I also want to install some electrical lighting. Do you think the man who's coming to fix the door could handle any of that? He said he was a handyman."

"Yeah, Ben can do just about anything you throw at him," Gabe said. "He's done work around the house for Meredith. I'm sure when he comes to fix the door, if you ask him, he can give you a price and maybe even add more suggestions for you."

Gabe grinned at her as he took a large bite of his bagel, peanut butter smearing the corner of his mouth. Morgan smiled back and picked up her napkin. She reached over and gently wiped the peanut butter away. It was a simple gesture, but it took them both by surprise. Dropping her hand, she hurriedly asked him how his day had gone while he was on the mainland.

"Pretty much as I expected. There were a few things that I needed to clear up with the lawyers regarding Uncle Dylan's estate." His eyes clouded over for a moment, but then he smiled gently and turned the conversation to Morgan. "What about you? Did you continue searching after I left?"

Morgan put down her coffee and reached into her pocket to pull out a small packet. "Yes, and thanks to Misty, I think I found something. It's not what the intruders were looking for, but I think they lost something in the process. Here, look at this." She pushed the packet over to him, not wanting to touch the necklace herself. Gently he unwrapped the cloth she had placed the pearl in.

"That's got to be the ugliest pearl I've ever seen." Gabe held the necklace up in the air looking at the pearl, his brow wrinkling with distaste.

"I know," Morgan agreed. "I can't even stand to touch it. Something is disturbing about it. I've never seen a pearl so dull and lackluster, not even one that's just been harvested. Black pearls are usually beautiful, but this one is...I don't know. Empty? Void?"

Even though Morgan struggled to describe her feelings, Gabe knew exactly what she meant; he was feeling it himself. Without a word, he put the necklace back in the cloth and wrapped it back up tightly, handing it back to Morgan. "Any idea where it came from?"

Morgan quickly told him her theory of Sirena losing the necklace while searching Meredith's office. He thought about it after she finished and had to agree she was right, but they still had no idea what Sirena might have been looking for.

"So, what are you going to do with the necklace? Are you going to give it to Jenny?"

Morgan was silent for a moment, contemplating his questions. Then she gave a slight shake of her head. "No, something is telling me to hang onto this. Maybe I'll confront Sirena myself with it at some point." Gabe didn't push the matter, he was learning to trust Morgan's judgment, and he was sure she was right. Maybe not so much about the necklace but the fact that at some point there would be a confrontation between the two women.

As if saying her name brought the woman to their doorstep, they heard a voice call out, and they looked up and saw Jenny coming around the corner of the house.

"I knocked on the front door but got no answer," Jenny said. "Then I remembered this courtyard and all the time Meredith spent in it. You wouldn't happen to have another cup there? That coffee smells heavenly."

Morgan held up her hand for Jenny to wait for a second and rushed into her workroom, coming back out a few seconds later with a clean cup. Jenny had made herself comfortable in one of the chairs and grabbed a bagel. Without a word, Morgan poured her coffee, adding the right amount of sugar and creamer that she remembered her friend liking. They were silent as Jenny enjoyed the first sips of her coffee.

"Did you find anything out when you cleaned up the office?" she finally asked as she put her cup down in the saucer, looking at Morgan.

Morgan and Gabe exchanged looks, but Morgan told Jenny they'd found nothing. The other woman seemed to sense something going on between the two of them, but Jenny held her tongue, not saying a word.

"Well, I have some news of my own." Jenny paused as if to make her next words more meaningful. "My partner didn't come into work today. When I drove around his house to see if he was okay, it didn't look like he was there last night, either. Stanley has just disappeared. I drove around the island looking for him, thinking maybe something was wrong, but there's no sign of him. And there's no sign of Sirena either."

Her words had the effect she thought they would, and the other two stared at her for a moment before they started asking questions.

The three of them went over all the possibilities of where Stanley or Sirena could have disappeared to, but Jenny had checked them all out, and the ones she hadn't checked out she had called, but still there was no sign of them.

Finally, Jenny glanced down at her watch, realizing she needed to get moving. She now had to do the work of two, and even though the island was small, it was a responsibility she didn't shirk. She thanked Morgan for the coffee and bagel and started to leave the courtyard. She hesitated before she turned the corner and looked back at her two friends sitting next to each other.

"I don't know what's going on, or what any of this means, but please be careful."

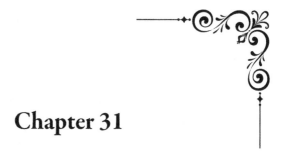

Chapter 31

Morgan and Gabe sat talking about Jenny's announcement. It was the loud cry of a peacock that made Morgan realize how much time they had spent talking.

"I need to kick you out, Gabe. I have to work on my book order to have it done on time for the client." When the man beside her looked like he would argue, she stopped him. "I'm sure you have things to do. Don't put off things for me. Didn't you say you had a group of kids who were expecting music lessons today? Go and play the Pied Piper; don't disappoint those kids. Seriously, I'll be tied up all day with this. I'm not leaving the house until it's done."

Gabe stood up, ready to argue with her, but she wasn't having any of it. Putting her hands firmly on his shoulders, she gave him a shove towards the walkway leading to the front of the house, the same one Jenny had just disappeared down. With a laugh, he agreed and then hesitated for a second.

"Why would you say Pied Piper?" he asked, smiling.

Morgan grinned back at him and gave a shrug of her shoulders. "The very first time I heard you playing the violin, I couldn't see you. You were swallowed up in the mist coming off the ocean. But I could hear you, and I felt like I wanted to follow the sound. Just like those children in the fairytale."

Gabe grinned back at her, not correcting her that the Pied Piper had played the flute, whereas he played the violin. He couldn't help but be charmed at the picture she painted with her words, and he was still smiling as he left.

Morgan didn't waste any time. She placed the leftover bagels and empty coffee cups on the tray, carrying it into the kitchen. She saw Misty was sitting in front of the door, soaking up the sunlight coming through the window. Knowing the cat would sleep for a couple of hours, she hurried to her workroom and closed the door behind her, barring the kitten from entering the room and causing havoc.

The hours passed quickly, interrupted by a few phone calls. One was from Jenny, checking in to make sure she was okay and report that she still had not found her partner or Sirena. Gabe checked in with her a few times, and they arranged to meet at the pizza shop for dinner. But it was the third interruption that captured Morgan's attention the most.

It was Winnie, calling from the museum. After a few pleasantries, she got right to the point.

"Morgan, I found something here that might interest you. It belonged to your aunt. To be honest, I don't remember her leaving it here, but it's yours now."

Morgan's interest was piqued, but she knew she couldn't leave in the middle of what she was doing. Winnie understood, telling her there was no hurry.

"It's been here for I don't know how long, so another day or two won't make a difference. You come when you get the chance. It will be here waiting for you."

Morgan assured the woman that she would be there at the first opportunity. Then she promptly got caught back up in the work at hand, pushing the conversation with the older woman to the back of her mind.

It wasn't until Morgan had to turn on the overhead light that she realized how late it had gotten. She had worked through lunch, only stopping once or twice for necessities and to give the kitten attention when she'd sat on the other side of the door howling.

Looking at the clock, she realized she had just enough time to take a quick shower before she needed to leave to meet Gabe at the pizzeria as arranged.

Finished with the shower, she threw on a pair of shorts and a casual top. She smiled to herself when she realized she hadn't dressed up since she'd arrived on the island. There were no meetings to attend or new clients to meet. Everything was being handled through the phone and the Internet, and she found she rather enjoyed doing business this way.

She started to walk out of the bedroom door and then looked down at the dresser and saw the wrapped piece of cloth that held the necklace she was coming to loathe. Morgan hesitated for a moment, not sure what to do about it. She didn't want to leave it in the house in case Sirena returned looking for it. With a disgusted look, Morgan picked up the necklace and put it in her pocket, pushing it down as far as it would go so she didn't have to be reminded of it. As she brought her hand out of her pocket, she reached for her own pearl necklace, as if her blue pearl could cleanse her of the ugly feeling she had after touching the black pearl.

Acting on impulse, she locked the cat in her bedroom just in case there were any more problems with break-ins. The last thing she wanted was for something to happen to Misty. Then she made her way downstairs. She hesitated at the base of the stairs, then noting the time, she decided to cut through the gardens rather than taking the long way.

Morgan made sure she locked the gates behind her as she went through each one of them. The peacocks seemed indifferent to her passing by, but Morgan called out a greeting to them, anyway. She had enjoyed looking out into the courtyard throughout the day, seeing the peacocks walking around.

When she arrived at the pizzeria, she found not only Gabe, but Jenny and Kathy, too. They had already ordered the food, and by mutual agreement, they kept the conversation light, talking about current events in the world. Morgan filled them in on some unusual places she had been over the years to restore old books. She'd encountered some characters along the way, and she had them in stitches laughing over some of the people she had worked for.

Their talking and laughter lasted long past the last piece of pizza, and it was not until the owner came over with the bill that they realized they were the last of the restaurant's patrons still there. Gabe quickly apologized for taking up the table for so long, but the owner waved his hand, dismissing the apology.

"It wasn't that busy, and you all were having such a good time. It's nice to see friends sharing time together like this. But I need to close, and you need to get home." Using a broom in his hand, he made as if to sweep them out the door, and with laughter the four left.

They each went their separate ways, still basking in the glow of friendship, not thinking of the dangers that had been intruding on the island. For one evening they had forgotten the problems and enjoyed each other's company.

It was as Morgan closed the first gate behind her that she remembered. The hair stood on the back of her neck, and there was a rustle in the bushes behind her. She quickly turned and saw a shape coming towards her. It was a large form, and she realized it was a man, but she couldn't make out his figure because he was clothed in a dark hoodie and long pants. The hood was over his head, covering most of his features. Morgan turned to run just as he reached out to grab her. She eluded him but when she reached the second gate and had to fumble with the lock, she knew it would only be seconds before he caught up with her.

But Morgan had security on her property that she didn't even know about. As she tried to open the second gate, her fingers shook, and she couldn't punch in the numbers correctly. She heard footsteps behind her and knew it was just a matter of seconds before he reached her.

Suddenly there was a loud screeching cry of multiple birds, furious at being disturbed. The birds did what was natural and attacked the intruder. They instinctively left Morgan alone and went after the man closing in on her.

She heard the man cry out in pain, then saw him raise his arm as if to swing at one bird.

"No," she cried out.

Then she realized another natural element was coming to her aid. The mist was developing quickly, hiding the birds and Morgan from the attacker's view. The man stumbled around, unable to see where he was going. Finally, he seemed to give up and retreat, running back the way he'd come, banging into things as he went. Morgan leaned against the gate with relief. Her weight swung it open, she had punched in the right numbers after all. The mist was thick, and she couldn't see anything behind her in the garden. She heard the birds retreat to their aviary as she firmly closed the gate behind her, hearing it click in place. The mist swirled around her feet but didn't obscure her view, and she hurried the rest of the way to the house.

She was just about ready to open the door to her aunt's office when she heard heavy footsteps coming down the pathway. In fright she turned, not prepared to confront whoever was coming this time.

"Morgan!"

Morgan gave a weak laugh as she recognized Gabe's voice. A second later, he burst through the mist and was standing in front of her.

"Are you okay?" Gabe put his hands on her shoulders, looking her over as if to reassure himself that she was unharmed.

"Yes, I'm fine, really. What are you doing here?"

"I'm not sure. I had a sudden urge to check on you, so I cut through some yards and came up the front of the house. I could hear the peacocks screaming in anger, and I knew something was wrong."

"Thank you. Thank you for following your instincts because something was very wrong. Somebody tried to grab me in the garden.

Those wonderful peacocks, those beautiful animals, saved me. You are absolutely right; they're the best security system anybody can have."

Morgan gave another weak laugh, trying to make light of what had happened.

But it was easy for Gabe to see she was shaken, and he opened the door, following her into the house.

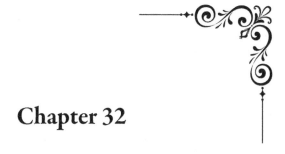

Chapter 32

Without a word, Gabe escorted Morgan to the great room. He forced her to sit down on the couch, wrapping a blanket around her shoulders. Only then did he speak.

"You sit here. Don't move, and just relax; I'm gonna go make you a hot cup of tea. I'll be right back."

Morgan nodded, but he didn't stick around long enough to see it. With his long legs moving fast, he went to the kitchen to make her the promised tea. Morgan couldn't help but grimace when she heard the makings of tea coming from the microwave. But it saved time, and it was only a couple minutes, and he was back in front of her pushing the hot tea into her hands.

"Your aunt always said hot tea with honey would fix everything."

Morgan grinned back at him, remembering the rest of what her aunt would say about hot tea and emergencies. "But if you really want it fixed, it needs a shot of whiskey."

Her words took Gabe by surprise, and then he burst out laughing. It was just what the two of them needed. Walking to a small cabinet, he opened it up with the knowledge of somebody who had been there before. Grabbing a bottle of whiskey, he added a healthy dose to Morgan's tea. She grinned back at him before taking a swallow, grimacing at the taste.

They were silent for a few moments while Morgan sipped the tea. Then they heard a commotion from upstairs, and Gabe jumped to his feet, ready to defend Morgan. She reached out and grabbed his hand to settle him, explaining there was nothing to fear.

"I closed Misty up in my bedroom. She's probably just figured out we're here and isn't happy about not being able to get out."

When she made a movement to get up, he pushed her back down on the couch. "You stay and finish your tea," he ordered. "I'll run upstairs and let the cat out."

A few seconds later, Misty rushed into the room, the hair on the back of her neck standing up as if she were ready to fight a battle. But when she saw Morgan, she settled down and jumped up on the couch next to her. Gabe entered the room at a slower pace.

He sat down next to Morgan and took her hand in his. "You ready to tell me what happened?"

Morgan scratched the kitten's head as Misty curled up in her lap and found she was ready to tell Gabe everything that had just happened. It didn't take long, and when she finished, she could feel the anger and tension coming off him through the hands that held her. But she had questions of her own and when she asked them, she felt Gabe sigh before he answered.

"The peacocks were the heroes, but there was another element that played a big factor; it was the mist," she told him. "Why does the mist show up so much, and always around me?"

"Think about it, Morgan. When does the mist show up? When you're upset? Afraid?"

"Oh please, tell me it's not another legend. Some good old-fashioned hard facts would be appreciated right now."

"I'm afraid I can't explain it Morgan, other than by legend. The Seavers have always been able to control the mist, bringing it to their defense when threatened. This was a gift the first mermaid gave to the first Seaver just as she disappeared into the sea."

Morgan closed her eyes and let her head fall back against the back of the couch. She didn't know what to believe. Her heart told her Gabe was telling the truth, but her mind was having a hard time accepting his words. It seemed awfully convenient that there was a legend for everything unexplained. But maybe it wasn't convenient; perhaps there was truth to the legends.

Gabe said nothing; he just let her sit. Reaching over, he took the now empty cup of tea away from her and carried it back to the kitchen. He deliberately stayed in the kitchen for a few minutes to give her time to come to grips with what he had said. When he returned, he found Morgan looking at him curiously.

"Your family plays a big part in these legends," she said. "I don't think you've told me everything, have you?"

But Gabe ignored her question and asked one of his own. "Do we call Jenny and let her know what happened?"

"Not tonight. There's nothing she can do anyway. Whoever it was won't return anytime soon. I'm sure of it." Morgan gave him a funny look, accepting that he would not answer her original question.

Gabe was silent for a moment, and then he agreed. Morgan was right; there would be no return from her attacker tonight. But he was taking no chances.

"Whether you like it or not, you have a houseguest tonight. I'll sleep down here on the couch. There's no sense in taking any chances."

Morgan didn't argue with him. She was grateful that she would not have to sleep in the house alone tonight. She could deal with her fears in the morning. But tonight, it was all too close to what had just happened.

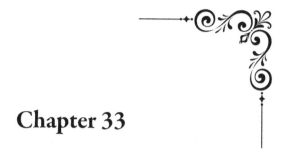

Chapter 33

Morgan woke the next morning to a quiet house. Even Misty had disappeared from the bedroom. Deciding to move quietly and quickly, she went to the bathroom to take her shower and get ready for the day. As she stood under the steaming water, she thought over the events of the night before. A chill ran down her back despite the hot water.

When she finished, she made her way downstairs and discovered where the kitten had disappeared to. During the night, she had abandoned Morgan and made her way downstairs to curl up with Gabe. Gabe had taken over the over-sized couch in the family room, which thankfully accommodated his height. During the night, he'd flipped over onto his stomach, and his hand now stretched out towards the floor. In the small of his back curled up and sleeping soundly was a kitten.

Morgan smiled at the picture and called softly to the kitten so she wouldn't wake Gabe. But the kitten had other ideas. She opened her eyes and then stretched, digging her claws into the small of Gabe's back.

"What the heck!" Gabe woke with a jerk, sitting up and wondering what was going on. Then he saw the culprit winding herself around Morgan's looking innocent. He shook a finger at her in a threatening manner, but the cat ignored him. Morgan could understand his frustration, and she scolded the kitten. She knew from experience just how sharp those tiny little claws were.

"Sorry about the rude awakening. But if I make coffee and cinnamon donuts, will that make up for it?" Morgan asked as she watched Gabe rub his hands over his face, trying to wake up. It was clear he wasn't the morning person that she was.

Twenty minutes later, they sat across the kitchen table from each other, finishing the last donut. They were discussing whether they should call Jenny to tell her about what happened the night before. Gabe was all for it, thinking she needed to write up a report, but Morgan was more hesitant. She knew Jenny had a lot on her plate. With a missing partner, that meant double the duty, at least until the police department sent in reinforcements. Morgan didn't want to add any more to her workload, especially when there was nothing she could do about it except for writing up a report.

"Seriously, Gabe, if we're careful and keep an eye on each other, we'll be doing the same thing Jenny would do. If something else happens, we'll say something to her, but let's let it ride for now. Wait and see what happens next."

Gabe shook his head, but he agreed with the stipulation that Morgan was not to be alone at any time during the day.

"And how do you suppose that's gonna happen? Are you planning on hiring a babysitter?" Morgan couldn't hide her sarcastic tone. She wasn't used to having someone around her all the time, and as much as she liked Gabe, she had a feeling it would get on her nerves pretty quickly.

"Consider me your babysitter. I have no classes today. The kids are on vacation, and we have canceled music classes for two weeks until everybody returns. We're stuck with each other. So, what's on the agenda?"

Even though Morgan had known Gabe for only a short period, she recognized the stubborn set of his jaw and the unflinching gaze. He would not back down from what he thought was right. With a sigh, Morgan realized he probably was right, and she gave in gracefully.

"To be honest, I had just planned on working here today. I still have another whole set of books that need my attention. Oh, and I promised Winnie that I would stop by the museum. She said she wanted to show me something. I want to do that before I get too involved in anything else."

"Perfect. How about if I drop you off at the museum? You'll be in the company of somebody else, and I can run home and get changed and ready for the day. I can pick you up in about an hour."

Morgan smiled back at him, understanding he was compromising. "That's perfect. I'm sure there's plenty to explore at the museum to keep me occupied for an hour or even more if you have a lot of things to do."

"Nope, an hour will be fine. I'll grab stuff for me to do while you're working in your office and we'll stay out of each other's hair for the rest of the afternoon. How does that sound?"

"Perfect. But I don't want you to feel like I'm ungrateful. I never would've thought you were in my hair, so to speak," Morgan protested.

"It's okay, Morgan." Gabe took a step towards her, touching her arm in a comforting manner. "I understand. You're used to being on your own. To be honest, I'm the same way; I like my own company. But I have to admit I'm enjoying your company too."

Before Morgan could answer him, her cell phone rang. It was Jenny checking in. Morgan told her friend she was okay, not bothering to tell her what had happened the night before.

"Just be careful today, Morgan. Stanley still hasn't shown up, and I haven't found Sirena either. I don't know if the two are connected or not, but I have a bad feeling."

"I promise. How soon before you have somebody coming in to help you?" Morgan asked.

Jenny assured her she had reinforcements that would be on the island by noon to relieve her and give her a break, but Morgan had a feeling Jenny would not take that break. This was her island, and she would make sure all the residents were safe.

"Stanley will have a lot of explaining to do to his partner," Gabe said as Morgan hung up the phone. He had heard the conversation and was shaking his head in disgust.

"You're right. Let me just grab my keys and we'll head out to the museum. That will give you time to get your stuff done too." Morgan left and returned within a few minutes with a set of keys. As they headed out, she locked the front door, thinking to herself that her Aunt Meredith had never locked the house up, and it was a shame that the peacefulness of the island was so disturbed.

Gabe used the car today even though he usually didn't, and it wasn't long before he was pulling up to the museum. Morgan assured him she would be fine, and he didn't argue. Instead, he watched as she got out of the car and entered the museum, not leaving until the door closed behind her.

"Good morning, Winnie," Morgan called out as she entered the museum. She heard a mumble from the back room, and a few moments later, the older woman joined her in the main lobby. The two exchanged pleasantries for a moment, and then Winnie commented on Stanley's disappearance. Morgan was taken aback for a moment, but then she realized the small island community kept no secrets. Plus, the fact that Jenny was Winnie's granddaughter and she probably had told her firsthand what had happened.

"Strange things are happening on the island, aren't they Winnie?"

"Stranger things happened before, and I'm sure things will happen again," the older woman replied. "It's just the cycle of the island. Now, I have something here for you that belonged to your aunt. Just give me a second and I'll find it."

Winnie changed the subject and turned away from Morgan before she could answer. While Winnie was searching for whatever she'd misplaced, Morgan wandered around the room. Just as before, she was drawn to the painting of the mermaids. Now that she knew the legend, she understood the picture and the hold it had on her. She was most interested in the second mermaid, the one whose fury was evident in the painting.

"There's something about that face," she mumbled to herself. "I know I've seen it before."

"Probably in some of those journals in your aunt's library." Winnie had come out of the backroom without Morgan realizing it, and her voice made Morgan jump nervously. "One of your ancestors loved to paint, and he was forever doodling in those journals." With a shake of her head, she turned back to the older woman.

"No, it's not from there, although I found some of those doodles. No, I've seen that face more recently, and I don't think it was in the painting or drawing. I don't know; it makes little sense." Morgan looked down at Winnie's hands and saw she was holding something. "Is that what you were looking for? What is it?"

"Yes, found it right where I put it." She held the object out to Morgan.

As she took it from her, Morgan realized it was a musical instrument, a small, miniature hand-carved recorder. She turned it over and saw whoever had made it had also engraved pictures on the backside of the recorder. Dancing dolphins, seahorses and coral were etched into the beautiful piece of wood.

"It's exquisite." Morgan looked at the other woman and smiled. "Did Meredith play it?"

Winnie burst out laughing at the question. Shaking her head, she explained. "Nope, your aunt used to say she couldn't play a note to save her life. The musical talent skipped a generation, she would tell me. And then she would boast at how well you played. I know she wanted you to have this."

Gently, Morgan reached out and took the instrument from her. Without giving it much thought, she raised it to her lips, playing the same tune she had heard Gabe play on the violin. When she finished, she looked at the other woman, who had a strange look on her face.

Morgan followed the direction of her gaze and saw the shimmering form of her Aunt Meredith standing near the painting.

But before either of the mortal women could say a word, Meredith smiled and disappeared.

"So, it's true. Your aunt's ghost is on the island," Winnie said matter-of-factly.

"You don't sound surprised. You almost sound like you expected it."

"Of course, I expected it. Meredith would never leave you alone until you were ready to be on your own here on the island. To be honest, there's always been a Seaver ghost here. Sometimes more than one."

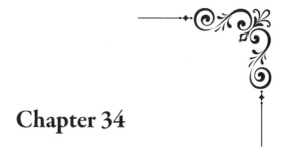

Chapter 34

It was almost anti-climactic. The next few days passed with nothing unusual happening except for everybody being nervous and walking on eggshells. Somehow Jenny had found out about Morgan's would-be attacker. It didn't take long before Kathy showed up at Morgan's house, backpack in hand, ready to stay with her new friend until it was over. When Morgan protested, Kathy merely said she didn't feel comfortable staying by herself while Jenny was out working. Morgan couldn't refuse when it was put like that, and for the time being, she had a houseguest.

With Kathy staying at the Seaver house, Gabe could attend to family duties. The lawyer had insisted on an additional meeting to go over the estate Uncle Dylan had left behind. "I can put them off, if you feel more comfortable, Morgan. I don't know why they're in such a rush."

Gabe, Morgan, and Kathy were in the courtyard watching the peacocks strut around. Gabe's friend Ben had left just a few moments before, taking the measurements of the area, promising to come up with a water feature that wouldn't take over the quaintness of the courtyard.

"Don't be silly," Morgan said. "And the lawyers are only following Dylan's wishes. Kathy is here with me, and there's been no sign of any trouble. So, go to your appointment and do what you must do. We'll be fine here," Morgan reassured him.

But what she didn't tell him was that she had found some signs of somebody around the house. They were subtle, and most people wouldn't have noticed it. But Misty had pointed out the footprints outside the shed where the bikes were stored. The cat's hair had stood on end, and she'd hissed at the small footprint. Morgan surmised it was Sirena who had been spying on her, but she couldn't prove anything, and there was no sense in getting everybody upset.

"We'll be fine, Gabe. As a matter of fact, it's a perfect excuse to stop by the museum and talk to my grandmother," Kathy added.

Gabe finally agreed, after getting both girls to promise to be careful. They watched him leave the courtyard, his shoulders slumped as if he were carrying a heavy weight. He had talked little about Dylan's disappearance into the sea, but Morgan knew he had accepted his uncle was gone. She didn't think he was ready for her to tell her what she'd seen the night before, but she would soon. She had been out on the widow's walk, looking down on the shore. The moonlight had been bright, and at first, she hadn't noticed the shimmering by the rocks. When she did notice, she waved a hand in greeting to her aunt, stopping mid-air when she realized there was a second figure standing by her aunt's side, holding her hand. The second figure was as familiar to her as her aunt, and he raised Meredith's hand in his so they could both wave at Morgan. The soul mates were together once again.

"He'll be fine once he gets all the legalities taken care of and can move forward. He had a good, healthy relationship with his uncle, and the memories he has will get him through." Kathy spoke softly, seeming to read Morgan's mind, jarring her from the moonlit memory.

Morgan returned her smile as the two of them watched Gabe disappear. "A trip to the museum is a great idea. I love talking to your grandmother, and there are so many unusual things there to look through."

Within ten minutes, they were walking towards the museum, happy to get some exercise. As they left the house, Morgan at the last minute had grabbed the small recorder and tucked it into the pocket of her sundress. She wanted to take it back to the museum and see if she could find any more information about it.

It delighted Winnie to see the two girls, and she put a temporarily closed sign on the door so she could spend uninterrupted time with her granddaughter and their new friend. Kathy and her grandmother quickly caught up on family stuff while Morgan wandered around the museum finding new things to look at. That was one thing that she loved about coming here; there was always something new to discover, and Winnie seemed to know the history of every object on display.

Today Winnie had gotten in a new box of small items an island resident had donated. The three of them spent the next hour going through each piece. Winnie knew what most of them were but was pleased when she found a few things she didn't have.

"How about if I get to work making up signs for these new items?" Winnie suggested, holding up a miniature sundial attached to a chain like what a pocket watch would have been. "You two girls can use the Internet and see if you can do any research on what these other items are. I'd like to have a history to go with each item when I put them on display."

Kathy and Morgan happily agreed to help out, eager for something different to do. It was a pleasant way to spend the day, and Winnie quietly ordered in lunch, not wanting to disturb the girls' work. They were on the last donated piece, having discovered information about the others when Morgan became restless. Leaving Kathy to continue working on the last article, Morgan got up and wandered around the museum. Before she knew it, she was standing in front of the painting, staring intently at the mermaids depicted on the canvas.

"Who are you?" she thought to herself as she stared at the artwork. "Got it!"

Kathy's shout brought her out of her musings, and she turned around to see the other girl doing a happy dance around the computer. Morgan walked back over to see what information her friend had found. Winnie joined them, ready to write things down to create information cards for the display.

With their chore finished, they spent a few more minutes with Winnie and then headed home. Kathy was exhilarated with her research, and Morgan understood Kathy shared a love of history with her grandmother. Regardless of Winnie's despairing of her gypsy ways, Morgan had a feeling that Kathy would be the one who took over the museum. Not Jenny, who had created deeper roots tying her to the island.

The two women had almost reached the Seaver house when Kathy realized she'd left her phone behind at the museum. Torn between retrieving the forgotten item and keeping her promise to Gabe, Kathy fidgeted at the walkway, causing Morgan to stop and look at her.

"What's up with you?" Morgan asked with a laugh.

"I can't believe it; I left my phone sitting on the counter at the museum."

"So, go back and get it. I'll be fine. Look, I'm fifteen steps away from the front door. You know as well as I do that Jenny will be upset if she can't reach you by phone. While you run back, I'll figure out what we're gonna have for dinner."

"Are you sure?" Kathy looked towards the house and then back in the direction of the museum. "I promised Gabe—"

"Go. The sooner you go, the sooner you'll get back. I promise not to tell Gabe you left me alone for ten minutes." Morgan gently gave Kathy a shove in the museum's direction, and after another moment of hesitation, Kathy nodded and headed off at a fast pace.

Morgan turned and headed to the house, taking a seat on one of the porch swings and looking out over the ocean. She sighed contently. "Finally, a few moments to myself," she whispered. Then she immediately felt guilty, but not guilty enough that she regretted the feelings.

MIST AT THE BEACH HOUSE

The wind coming off the ocean seemed to pick up with intensity, and Morgan looked out towards the dunes. She stuck her hands in her pockets, absentmindedly fingering the miniature recorder. In the other pocket, she could feel the small piece of cloth holding the black pearl. She'd been carrying it with her since she found it, not knowing why, but not wanting to leave it unattended.

As she watched the shoreline, a woman dressed in a dark flowing sundress made her way down the dune towards the shore. There was something about the woman that drew Morgan's attention, and she got to her feet without even realizing it. She could feel her anger building as she realized the woman had come from the direction of Meredith's shed.

Letting the anger take control of her, Morgan raced down the steps heading towards the shore, intent on following the woman, determined to question her to find out who she was and demand an answer to what she wanted.

Chapter 35

Morgan had no idea why she was so intent on catching up with the strange women, but she felt driven to reach her before she disappeared. Morgan had seen her before, but she couldn't place her. As she tried to think of where she'd seen her before, Morgan began to doubt herself, wondering if she was mixing up a real person with the painting she was so entranced with.

Morgan gave no thought about safety; she forgot about the attack in the garden and the murder of her aunt. She was driven to find her answers, and she thought this woman might have them. There had been too many strange things happening around her since she had returned to Pearl Island. Things that couldn't be explained away with talks of legends. Crimes had been committed by live humans in the present day. These things she understood and wanted justice for.

The woman kept a steady pace ahead of Morgan, her black dress snapping in the wind. She moved with purpose, not hampered by the shifting sand as she walked. Morgan called out to her, but she didn't slow down. Maybe she hadn't heard Morgan over the sound of the waves. The cry of the seagulls circling the area and watching the beach below seemed to be a warning of danger. The wind picked up even more than it what it had been when she was on the porch, and the sand crystals stabbed at her face like tiny little pinpricks. Morgan's hair blew wildly into her face, and she could see the aqua streaks mixing in with the rest of her black hair like a flag of warning.

When the woman approached the rock outcropping, she turned and disappeared from Morgan's view. Morgan hesitated for just a moment, and the wind let up at the same time, allowing the skirt of her sundress to rest against her leg. Morgan jumped in shock from the intense cold coming from her pocket. It felt like an ice cube rested against her skin.

"What in the world?" Coming to a complete stop, Morgan reached into her pocket and pulled out the piece of cloth that held the pearl she'd found in the house.

As she unwrapped the pearl with her other hand, the wind picked back up and grabbed the piece of cloth, pulling it from Morgan's grasp. Morgan didn't even bother trying to rescue it as it was taken in the strong gust. Instead, she held the chain with two fingers as if it was something putrid. The pearl was no longer lackluster. Now it was as black as coal, tiny specks glistening in the center. As she held the chain up, it swung in the air as if the wind was trying to steal it from her fingers. With her other hand, she reached up to her throat to reassure herself her own pearl was still in place. As she felt the warmth of her own pearl against her throat, Morgan felt a strong sense of comfort. The wind blew the chain in her hand, making the black pearl twirl as if it had a power of its own. With a disgusted shudder, she shoved the necklace back in her pocket and felt it settle to the bottom of the fabric. Pulling her hand back out of her pocket, she touched the miniature recorder with her other hand and felt a sudden burst of strength.

"It's time to find out who you are, mystery woman," Morgan muttered to herself. She stood straighter, smoothing the fabric of her dress around the pocket, and as she moved forward, the wind picked back up.

The waves were getting rough, and the air seemed to crackle with tension as if a storm was approaching. Morgan neared the rocks, and she hesitated for a moment, Gabe's warnings coming to mind. Had she been foolhardy to rush off without somebody with her?

"It's too late for that now." Drawing in a deep breath, she reached up and held her own necklace for a moment, as if drawing courage from it. Then she followed the woman around the rock outcropping and came to a dead standstill.

"You! What are you two doing here?"

Chapter 36

Morgan stared at the two, standing in front of her. The two who'd been missing for days, the two the whole island had been searching for.

"Surprised to see us, Morgan?" Sirena's voice was filled with a sickening sweetness in direct contrast to the threatening manner of Stanley's stance beside her.

"Not really. I think you two are behind a lot more of what's been happening on this island than most people realize. And you know more about my aunt's death than you'll ever admit." With her hands on her hips, Morgan stood tall, not letting Stanley intimidate her with his height and size.

Sirena laughed at her reply. "So, you're smarter than I thought. Yeah, we're behind a lot of it—"

"Enough!"

For a moment, Morgan had forgotten about the woman she'd followed down the beach, but as her voice cracked with sharpness across the wind with sharpness, it all came back to Morgan. She turned her attention to the woman as she moved next to the others. Now she was facing the three of them.

"I know you. We met at my aunt's memorial service. I know you from somewhere else..."

"Yes, we've met in person, but if you think hard, you know where else you know me from." With a simple movement, the woman raised her hands above her head.

And in that instant, Morgan knew precisely where she'd seen her before. She was identical to the mermaid in the painting. The mermaid, who if the legend was to be believed, was the one who had destroyed the love between Morgan's ancestor and the other mermaid.

Common sense told Morgan everything was crazy, but as she stared into the cold eyes of Cora, she knew in her heart the legend was real, and she was facing an evil more significant than anything she'd ever encountered before.

"Give me back what is mine." Sirena's demand interrupted Morgan's thoughts as she turned her attention back to the other woman. Her long curls were tangled in the wind, and there was a desperation about her that Morgan didn't understand. Then it clicked. It was Sirena who had left the pearl behind in Morgan's house, and she wanted it back.

Morgan had a few questions of her own before she would admit she had the pearl with her. "It was you who searched my house. Why?"

But before Sirena could answer, Stanley laughed like a madman and took a menacing step towards Morgan. Sirena put her hand out, touching his arm, stopping his movement. Morgan watched, fascinated, when Stanley looked down at the beautiful woman as if under her spell.

But he was the one who answered her question. "We searched your house more than once. And you never knew it. I had you within my reach one night until those stupid birds got in my way."

It took Morgan a moment to figure out what he was talking about, but then she remembered the dark night when she had walked to the garden only to be chased by somebody. The peacocks had saved her that night, and as she stared at the man, she felt that same fear she felt in the garden. She'd been foolish to come here; she wasn't safe. There were no peacocks along the beach to save her this time. With that realization, she understood this was probably exactly what had happened to her aunt as well; she had followed her killer without thinking of the consequences.

MIST AT THE BEACH HOUSE

"Which of you killed my aunt?" Morgan looked back and forth between Sirena and Stanley, knowing in her heart it had been one of them.

Cora had been silent as she watched the three of them interact, but now it was she who stepped forward, and as she did, the wind and the waves intensified, and lightning flashed across the sky.

"Give Sirena back what is hers."

Morgan felt a movement on her hand and ran her finger across the shell of her pearl ring. While she had been confronting those in front of her, the shell had opened, exposing the pearl. Instinctively, she shoved her hand into her pocket to conceal the ring from view of the others. Her hand touched the coldness of Sirena's necklace.

"Why is her necklace so important? And why should I give it back to her?" Morgan demanded of Cora.

Cora's face filled with rage, and she took another step towards Morgan. But Morgan held her ground. She knew she should be afraid of Cora, but she wanted answers, and that outweighed her sense of preservation.

Cora's expression turned from rage to smugness as she looked at something behind Morgan. Before Morgan could turn to see what she was looking at, she heard shouts behind her, recognizing the voices of Gabe, Jenny, and Kathy. She looked back at Cora and realized their timing had put them in danger.

Cora smiled dangerously; she had been given a weapon to use against Morgan. "Give me the necklace." She held out her hand, expecting Morgan to obey her.

"No."

The sand swirled around Cora like a miniature tornado, and Stanley took a step back, suddenly fearful. Even Sirena eyed Cora hesitantly. The woman in black's anger was palpable. Then she seemed to get a hold of herself, and the sand settled.

Raising her hands above her head again, she pointed her fingers at Morgan's friends racing towards her. "Save your friends and give me the necklace."

To prove her point, she made a jerk of one hand, and a huge wave crashed against the shore close to where Gabe and the women were running. Morgan hesitated; did she have the right to put her friends in danger? Morgan knew now that Cora could control more than just herself. Somehow, she had control of Sirena, Stanley, and the sea. And she had a feeling the repulsive black pearl helped her keep control of the two who stood by her side. That had to be why she was so determined to have Morgan return it.

Then Morgan saw something else. Something the others couldn't see. Morgan watched as Meredith appeared. Her aunt made a motion at Morgan, and Morgan immediately understood what her aunt wanted her to do.

Grasping hold of the necklace, she pulled it out of her pocket, holding it up in the air for Cora to see. Sirena immediately took a step towards her as if to grab the necklace, and Morgan instinctively twisted. But the movement was enough to cause the miniature recorder in her pocket to fall out. It had caught on the chain of the necklace and was hanging on to the edge of her pocket.

"No!" screamed Cora.

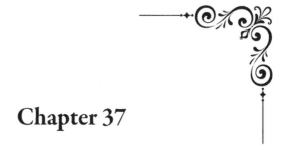

Chapter 37

M organ looked at Cora, who had her eyes fixed on the recorder lying on the sand. She seemed frozen by its appearance. Then she turned her head to glare at the shimmering form of Meredith.

This was the chance Morgan needed, and she didn't waste it. Instinctively, she grabbed the recorder and raced to the outcropping of rocks. She stood next to the largest of the rocks and grabbed a small rock lying on top. Then she put the necklace on the surface of the rock and, with all her might, brought the smaller rock down with force onto the black pearl. Her movement caught Cora's attention, but she was too late to stop the swing of Morgan's arm. The rock smashed onto the pearl, crushing it into pieces.

Sirena screamed out as if in pain, and Stanley crumpled to the ground as if released from the rope that had been holding him up. The two of them looked back and forth between Morgan and Cora, waiting for their reaction. When it happened, they were all speechless.

Cora's fury was overwhelming, and the sand rose up from the ground, screening her from view from the moment. But then the wind shifted, blowing the sand away from Cora. Now Morgan could see Sirena clutching at Cora as if pleading to the other woman. With a swift arch of her arm, Cora pushed Sirena away, and the upcoming wave caught her around the younger woman's feet, dragging her out to the depths of the ocean, her hair swirling in the waves. As Sirena disappeared, Stanley collapsed. It was as if something had released him, and he looked around him, confused. But then his eyes focused on the same thing Morgan was now watching. Meredith had walked to stand next to her niece.

"No, no, it's not possible! I killed you myself, you can't be here," Stanley screamed. Then he turned and ran away from the others as if being chased by something evil.

Cora was now staring at Meredith, speechless with anger.

"It's over, Cora. Go back to the sea," Meredith told the other woman quietly.

"It's not over. I destroyed your sister. I destroyed you. I will destroy your niece. Then the Seavers will be gone, and the island will be mine."

Cora stepped towards the two Seaver women, standing defiantly in front of her, but stopped as if she'd walked into a wall. Shaking, she took a step back and glared at Meredith, demanding to know what was going on.

"You made a mistake sending others to do your work. If you had been there, you would have seen what happened when I was killed," Meredith said. "You would have seen that I gave up my life willingly to protect my niece and the island, just as Seavers have been protecting the island for generations. Your hatred can't win against this kind of love, Cora. Not now, not ever."

By now, the others were just a few steps away, and Morgan heard Kathy gasp. She must be able to see Meredith. Jenny didn't stop; she kept running intent on stopping Stanley before he could get away again.

Gabe reached out and grabbed Morgan's hand, joining forces with her and Meredith as they stood between Cora and the island. Together the three of them took a step forward, and Cora took a step backward. They continued to walk until Cora reached the edge of the water. The four of them stared at each other, at an impasse.

Then, without realizing what she was doing, Morgan brought her hand out of her pocket, showing Cora the ring. "Go back to where you came from, Cora. Leave Pearl Island alone," Morgan demanded.

And then she lifted the recorder to her lips, instinct telling her to play the melody that she knew so well. Cora stared at the recorder as if it held some power over her. Morgan inhaled and began to play the instrument. Her fingers' movement held Cora's attention. Morgan finished the tune and stared at her opponent.

It took a few moments for Cora to break out of the trance-like state the music had put her in. During that time, Morgan and Meredith had walked forward, close enough to push the woman into the sea if they had to. Cora paused for a moment as if trying to decide if she wanted to continue the battle. Then she gave a shrug as if nothing mattered to her, and she turned to Morgan and sneered.

"We'll meet again. When you least expect it. This isn't over, but it will be soon. In the meantime, I'd watch your back and watch out for your friends."

Gracefully, Cora turned away from them and walked into the water. When she turned back to look at her enemies, she couldn't see them. A fine mist had engulfed them. With a hysterical laugh, she dove into the water, and the seas calmed.

Chapter 38

O nce Cora disappeared entirely, so did the mist. Morgan felt a soft, gentle touch of somebody pushing the hair out of her face, and when she looked to her side, she saw a slight shimmer, and then Meredith was gone.

"I don't know what just happened, but I'm thankful you're okay." Gabe wrapped her in his arms, giving her the support she hadn't realized she needed.

Kathy raced down the sand next to them, demanding to know what was going on. "Do we send out the rescue boats? Two women are lost in the water."

"They won't find anything. Sirena and Cora are gone. Jenny can make a report, but I think she's got her hands full right now." Gabe looked at Kathy and shook his head as he answered her.

The three of them looked down the beach and saw Jenny half dragging, half pushing her old partner towards them. He was wearing handcuffs and seemed half-crazed with fear. As Jenny approached, they could hear him saying repeatedly, "I killed her, I killed her."

Over the next hour, the beach in front of Morgan's house was full of activity. Jenny had called in help, and the police from the mainland had arrived to take Stanley into custody. Jenny had also notified the Coast Guard of the disappearance of two women into the ocean, but she had made no effort to go out and help them look for the missing women.

Winnie appeared, notified of the activity on the beach, and took both of her granddaughters under her wing. Giving comfort to Kathy, who still didn't understand all that she had seen, and praising Jenny for her role in capturing Stanley, Winnie's calm presence kept her granddaughters focused on the here and now. When it was time for the Colbrights to leave, Winnie came to stand in front of Morgan.

Taking her hands, she looked deep into Morgan's eyes. "You have survived this battle, Morgan. But I think you know as well as I do, it's not over. It won't be until Keyna and Cora confront each other one final time. Now, I will do as my ancestors have done, and I'll record this battle. Just as Gabe will stay here by your side and help you. We each have our place in the island's future. We need to work together to ensure the safety of Pearl Island and those who call it home." As she finished speaking, she looked down at the ring on Morgan's hand and smiled as the shell closed back around the pearl until Morgan would need it again.

Mist at the Beach House
End of Book one of six
Next: Mist across the Waves

I hope you enjoyed this book. If you did, please leave an honest review on the site you purchased it from.

Interested in the legend behind the story? If you would like to read "Legend of the Mist" please signup for my newsletter at www.VictoriaLKWilliams.com[1]

In the comments write Mermaid, and I will send you a copy!

Name Origins
Morgan: from the shore of the sea / Celtic
Meredith: protector of the seas / Celtic
Dylan: son of the seas / Welsh
Keyna: a jewel / Irish
Cora: seething pool / Scottish
Sirena: siren, enchantress / Greek
Gabriel: messenger, the strength of God / Greek
Erwinia (Winnie): Friend of the Sea / English
Jenny: White Wave / Celtic
Katherine (Kathy): pure, clear / Irish
Seaver: fierce stronghold / Anglo-Saxon

Don't miss out!

Visit the website below and you can sign up to receive emails whenever Victoria LK Williams publishes a new book. There's no charge and no obligation.

https://books2read.com/r/B-A-VGGF-OXLEB

BOOKS 2 READ

Connecting independent readers to independent writers.

Did you love *Mist at the Beach House*? Then you should read *Whispered Voices*[2] by Victoria LK Williams!

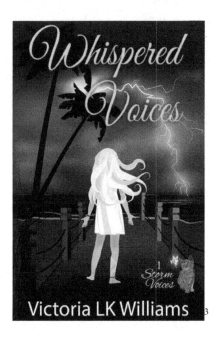

Whispered Voices, *Storm Voices 1*

A close call with nature gives Mac more than an feathered scar. She now has the ability to hear the thoughts of a killer. A fairy kiss or a curse? Mac needs to find out and time is running out before the murderer strikes again. Can she clear her best friend and stop another murder?

Read more at www.victorialkwilliams.com.

---

2. https://books2read.com/u/m2o2O6

3. https://books2read.com/u/m2o2O6

Also by Victoria LK Williams

A Beach House Mystery
Mist at the Beach House

Citrus Beach Mysteries
Murder for Neptune's Trident
Scent of a Mystery
Murder at the GeoCache
Runaway for Christmas
Tank Full of Trouble
The Flapper Caper
Borrowed, Blue, Dead
Trouble Has A Tail
Citrus Beach Mystery: Box Set: Books 1,2,3

Mrs. Avery's Adventures
Killer Focus
Final Delivery
The Dummy Did It

Sister Station Series
Now Arriving
Now Departing

Storm Voices
Whispered Voices
Deceptive Voices
Lost Voices

Tattle-Tale Mystery Novellas
The Toy Puzzle

Standalone
Cozy Christmas Collection

Watch for more at www.victorialkwilliams.com.

About the Author

Victoria believes that not everything can be answered by science. Faith and nature play a huge part in finding answers. Answers that often start with "what if".

*In her **Storm Voices** series, she wondered what would happen if you could hear the killers plans before they happen? And what if nature played a part in helping you solve the crime? With a love for gardening and watching lightning storms, the answers came to her enough to keep asking more questions and create a new series.*

*Currently, a new paranormal mystery series is in the draft stage: think murder, a ghost, and sea legends. Now start looking for the **Beach House Mystery Series**.*

Victoria also writes clean woman's fiction, with a touch of romance and a sprinkling of humor **Sister Station Series**. She also has two cozy Mystery Series **Citrus Beach Mysteries** and **Mrs. Avery's Adventures**.

She can often be found writing from her South Florida home, looking into her garden, watching the birds and squirrels fight over their next meal, while she writes. Her two cats, Miss Marple, and Fletch, often join her at the desk and each has their assigned spot. Victoria's not sure they are there to supervise her writing or watch the birds.

Victoria and her husband of 36 years share a love of gardening, and together they have written a gardening handbook for Florida gardeners.

Read more at www.victorialkwilliams.com.

Sun, Sand & Stories Publishing

About the Publisher

Books by our author, Victoria LK Williams have a tropical twist to them. Her characters are from the south, or are now in the south, but they all share a love of sun, sand & stories!

We are also pleased to offer the book **Pocket Guide to Florida Landscaping**, by *Donald R Williams*.

Made in the USA
Columbia, SC
26 May 2021

38550108R00114